**THE WOMAN WHO
WROTE THE BIBLE**

Jewish Latin America Series
ILAN STAVANS, SERIES EDITOR

The Jewish Latin America Series, relaunched in 2024, will introduce Jewish Latin American culture to a broad English-language readership. Through high-caliber translations as well as original English-language editions, it aims to open up a field of study by publishing classics as well as contemporary novels, memoirs, biographies, story collections, poetry, and anthologies. The series will map out the extraordinary creativity of the Jewish community in Latin America, from colonial times to the present, in a region far more diverse than is usually imagined.

Also available in the Jewish Latin America Series:

Otrarse: Ladino Poems by Juan Gelman, edited and translated by Ilan Stavans
I Am of the Tribe of Judah: Poems from Jewish Latin America, edited by Stephen A. Sadow
Yiddish South of the Border: An Anthology of Latin American Yiddish Writing, edited by Alan Astro
Like a Bride and Like a Mother by Rosa Nissán
Secrecy and Deceit: The Religion of the Crypto-Jews by David M. Gitlitz
The Martyr: Luis de Carvajal, A Secret Jew in Sixteenth-Century Mexico by Martin A. Cohen
Losers and Keepers in Argentina: A Work of Fiction by Nina Barragan
The Collected Stories of Moacyr Scliar by Moacyr Scliar
The Book of Memories by Ana María Shua, translated by Dick Gerdes
The Jewish Gauchos of the Pampas by Alberto Gerchunoff

MOACYR SCLIAR

THE WOMAN WHO WROTE THE BIBLE

A COMEDY OF TRULY BIBLICAL PROPORTIONS

INTRODUCTION BY **ILAN STAVANS**
TRANSLATED BY **HEATH WING**

UNIVERSITY OF NEW MEXICO PRESS | ALBUQUERQUE

Original Portuguese edition © 1999 by Moacyr Scliar
University of New Mexico Press English edition © 2026 by arrangement
with Straus Literary in association with Literarische Agentur Mertin Inh.
Nicole Witt e. K., Frankfurt am Main, Germany
English Translation © 2026 by Heath Wing
Introduction © 2026 by Ilan Stavans
All rights reserved. Published 2026
Printed in the United States of America

ISBN 978-0-8263-6931-4 (paper)
ISBN 978-0-8263-6932-1 (ePub)

Library of Congress Control Number: 2025945504

Founded in 1889, the University of New Mexico sits on the traditional homelands of the Pueblo of Sandia. The original peoples of New Mexico—Pueblo, Navajo, and Apache—since time immemorial have deep connections to the land and have made significant contributions to the broader community statewide. We honor the land itself and those who remain stewards of this land throughout the generations and also acknowledge our committed relationship to Indigenous peoples. We gratefully recognize our history.

Excerpt from *The Book of J* © 1990 by David Rosenberg and Harold Bloom. Used by permission of Grove/Atlantic, Inc. Any third-party use of this material, outside of this publication, is prohibited.

Cover illustration: *King Solomon's Wives Lead Him into Idolatry*, 1668 by Giovanni Battista Venanzi.
Designed by Felicia Cedillos
Composed in Arno Pro

CONTENTS

VII   INTRODUCTION. THE MAGICAL MOMENT
                 ILAN STAVANS

XXI   TRANSLATOR'S NOTE

1   THE WOMAN WHO WROTE THE BIBLE

135   CONTRIBUTORS

INTRODUCTION

THE MAGICAL MOMENT

ILAN STAVANS

> "Send us the cure—the affliction we already have."
> —SHOLOM ALEICHEM

DIASPORISM

"We live through countless moments, yet it is one moment, a single one, that casts the entire inner world into turmoil, the magical moment when, as Stendhal described it, the internal inflorescence, steeped in every kind of fluid, crystallizes." So states Stefan Zweig, among the most widely read writers of the first half of the twentieth century, in his novella *Confusion* (1927).

My friend Moacyr Scliar often talked about that elusive moment, its flash appearance, and the possibility of us irrevocably missing it. The magical moment is when, having absorbed the contradictions of the world outside, the creative spark inside us coalesces. If and when it succeeds, the result is radical, warranting a reinterpretation of reality. Scliar lived for those moments, turning them into novels, essays, stories, newspaper columns (called *crónicas* in Portuguese), and more.

I met Scliar for the first time in his native Porto Alegre. It was 1986 and I was traveling through Argentina and Brazil, intent on learning how their respective Jewish communities had developed since colonial times. Having read a handful of his novels in Portuguese, I sent him, out of the blue, a letter in advance. He responded promptly, inviting me for coffee as soon as I arrived in town. It was the beginning of a decades-long conversation that wasn't only epistolary. The happiest incarnation was when we traveled from one coast of the

United States to another, on a literary tour, with appearances as a duo in theaters where we engaged in lively public conversations.

The topics ranged from how Maimonides, among the most illustrious thinkers in Jewish culture, attempted, in twelfth-century Cordoba, in his philosophical book *The Guide for the Perplexed* (c. 1190), to reconcile the Bible and Aristotle; the fin de siècle German culture of Franz Kafka, Walter Benjamin, Gershom Scholem, Franz Rosenzweig, and Hannah Arendt; and the beautifully crafted Russian stories of Isaac Babel, who wrote under Soviet rule. But mostly we talked about Jewish Latin America, where we both came from. I mentioned Jacobo Timerman, the outspoken Argentine journalist responsible for the memoir *Prisoner Without a Name, Cell Without a Number* (1981), about the repression, especially the Jewish *desaparecidos*, during his country's military junta. In response, he would bring up Clarice Lispector, the masterful Ukrainian-Brazilian novelist of *Hour of the Star* (1977) and scores of other books.

These conversations, still vivid in my mind, addressed countless topics, principally what it meant to be Jewish in Latin America and, broadly, in the successive diasporas, from the Babylonian one after the destruction of the Second Temple in Jerusalem in the year 70 CE, to the collapse of cosmopolitan Jewish culture in Germany before the Holocaust and, nearer us, the culture of American Jews at the outset of the twenty-first century.

Although neither Scliar nor I were Zionists, I had lived in Israel in successive periods and he visited it regularly. Yet, as we discussed the issue on stage, the two of us rejected the idea of *alliyah* (in Hebrew, עֲלִיָּה). The word means "ascendance," as if exile (גלות, *galut*), life in the diaspora, was a lesser and unworthy form of existence. What I enjoyed about Scliar's oeuvre is the way his characters thrived on being different in Rio Grande do Sul, in the southernmost part of Brazil, bordering Uruguay on one side and Argentina on the other, where his Yiddish-speaking immigrant parents, along with many other Ashkenazic Jews in Brazil, settled.

In fact, I remember us often talking about "Diasporism," an antidote to Zionism in which memory is the essential tool nurturing Jewish life. A subject we often explored in front of our audiences was Stefan Zweig, who, along with his second wife, Lotte Altmann, died in Petrópolis, a German town north of Rio de Janeiro. Having escaped the Nazis, this Austrian-Jewish author of novels, stories, and biographies of Mary, Queen of Scots; Erasmus of Rotterdam; and

Ferdinand Magellan, among others, wrote a beautiful book about his host country, *Brazil, Land of Tomorrow* (1941), in which he suggested that cosmopolitanism, at a crossroads in the age of Adolf Hitler and Josef Stalin, might be revived in South America.

Not long after that, he and Altmann committed suicide by a barbiturate overdose, so deep was the depression they felt over the advance of Nazism on the European stage. Scliar was riveted by the way Zweig united the Old World and the New, stressing a continuity he himself constantly wrote about. In 1993, Philip Roth, another Jewish author Scliar cherished (he loved *Portnoy's Complaint* [1969]), published the novel *Operation Shylock*, about a doppelgänger, also called Philip Roth, whose task is to repatriate Israeli Jews to Poland because, in his eyes, Zionism has failed and Poland's economy, in shatters after the collapse of Communism in the USSR and the fall of the Berlin Wall, desperately needs a capitalist jolt. Somehow, Roth's tongue-in-cheek scenario was a continuation of Zweig's belief that Jewish cosmopolitanism only flourishes in the diaspora.

Scliar joked about an elderly lady sitting on a park bench in Tel Aviv with her young grandson, speaking to him in Yiddish. A bunch of people nearby approach them, launching into a diatribe: "You shouldn't be speaking to him in Yiddish, the language of the galut," they admonish, "but in Hebrew, the language of Israel." To which the lady responds: "But I want him to know he is Jewish." Scliar laughed. Life in Israel, he commented, is not without suffering. Just look at the intractable conflict between Israelis and Palestinians. Yet he preferred to see himself as part of a wandering people. By chance, his family emigrated to Brazil. And there, they not only thrived but enjoyed untrammeled freedom. Yes, during holiday prayer, Scliar yearned for a Promised Land. Yet yearning alone was sufficient, since it signaled that life is incomplete, in need of mending.

These emotions are ubiquitous in Scliar's work. He seems to have been struck quite often by that magical moment. Over the years, he satisfied my hunger for his new work, which periodically arrived in my mailbox: a new novel, an anthology, or Xeroxes of the crónicas he published in the Porto Alegre newspaper *Zero Hora*. And he sent me Spanish translations of *The Centaur in the Garden* (1980), arguably his most famous novel. I loved it. Its protagonist is Guedali Tartakovsky, a child of a Russian-Jewish immigrant couple of Rio Grande do Sul, who is bullied by his peers, both Jews and gentiles, because of his appearance. Yet Scliar empathizes with him, exploring his quest as an outsider. In characteristically straightforward humor and an unconvoluted style, the novel, which portrays the Jewish body as a monstrosity in need of acceptance, investigates Jewish–gentile relations. I also loved *Max and the Cats* (1981), about a Jewish boy in Germany during the Second World War who, escaping the Nazis, traverses the ocean on a small boat with a frightening, giant jaguar. And *The Strange Nation of Rafael Mendes* (1983), dealing with the plight of New Christians in Brazil, a land that, during the colonial period, became a magnet for converso Jews escaping the Portuguese Inquisition. (Some of the first settlers in New York in 1654, then called New Amsterdam, were Dutch-speaking Sephardic refugees from Brazil.)

I, too, sent Scliar my books, accompanied by epistolary disquisitions on my own intellectual journey. Our connection deepened, to such degree that when he died in 2011, I felt utterly alone without my beloved diasporic interlocutor.

ODRADEK

Born in Porto Alegre in 1937, Moacyr Scliar came of age in an immigrant enclave, Bom Fim (in Portuguese, "Good End"), largely populated, starting in the 1920s, by Yiddish-speaking Jewish immigrants from the Pale of Settlement in Central and Eastern Europe and their descendants. (His parents were from Bessarabia, which bounded by the Dniester River on the east and the Prut River on the west, is known today as Moldova.) Bom Fim had five synagogues: Centro Israelita, Linat Hatzedeck, Beit Lubavitcher, Maurício Cardoso Society (known as the Poilisher Farband), and União Israelita de Porto Alegre, built in 1910, the oldest synagogue in Brazil. Scliar took me to visit several of them. Likewise, the neighborhood features the Hebrew Society, the Cultural Club, and the Israeli Federation of Rio Grande do Sul, and houses the National Museum of Jewish Migrations.

Scliar attended a Yiddish school in 1943, and then, in 1948, he transferred to Colégio Rosário, completing high school in Julio de Castilhos State High School. Depending on the day, it was a rhapsodic transition or an agonizing one, going from a mostly Jewish environment like Bom Fim to an educational system where he interacted daily with Non-Jewish Brazilians. In no time he learned about the nation's profound economic, social, and political inequalities.

The immigrant mentality at Scliar's home made him hesitate, at first at least, to embark on a literary career. His parents made it clear that he needed a reliable profession to support himself and his future family—that is, one bringing in a steady income. For him and other young Brazilian Jews of the second generation, that meant a safe path in business or medicine. Consequently, he enrolled in medicine at the Federal University of Rio Grande do Sul, the largest public academic institution in the region. It was 1955, a year of turmoil after the end of Getúlio Vargas's dictatorial regime. A decade of relatively democratic tranquility would follow, interrupted by a military coup that established what is known as the Fifth Brazilian Republic.

He graduated from the Federal University of Rio Grande do Sul's Faculty of Medicine in 1962. Looking back at his medical training, he stated in an interview, "My work as an attending physician involved going to the impoverished neighborhoods in a Jeep or an old ambulance, where almost all the calls came from. What I saw in those shacks horrified me: sometimes there were five, six, ten people crammed into a small, stuffy, smelly shack. I had never had such a close encounter with poverty, not at the Santa Casa, the Pantheon Sanatorium, or the São Pedro Hospital. It was appalling, brutal." A few of his first stories appeared in *O Bisturi*, a newspaper affiliated with the Samento Leite Academic Center. His debut novel, *Histórias de un medico en formacão* (Story of a Doctor in Training, 1962), still untranslated, is equally autobiographical. It signaled a combined passion: As in the cases of Anton Chekhov and William Carlos Williams, medicine stimulated his literary endeavors, and vice versa.

One of his best novels, still unavailable in English, is *A majestade do Xingu* (The Majesty of Xingu, 1997). It tells the fictionalized odyssey of real-life physician Noel Nutels, considered the father of Brazilian public health. Born in Russia, Nutels immigrated to Pernambuco in 1921, at the age of eight. A left-wing intellectual, he joined the Indian Service in the 1940, devoting his life to Brazil's indigenous population. He died in 1973. Scliar's comedic narrative, set in a small shop in Bom Retiro, a neighborhood in São Paulo, is told from the viewpoint of a friend of Nutels's, who lies in a hospital bed in intensive care. Spanning several decades, the story explores the work of Nutels with the Xingu tribe. I remember when Scliar sent me a copy. I read it with immediate curiosity. It reminded me of a lesser-known novel by Mario Vargas Llosa called *The Storyteller* (1987), about Saúl Zuratas, an anthropology student and Sephardic Jew in Lima, Peru, who does the same: abandons modern life to join the Machiguengas, becoming their "griot," a keeper of their collective memory.

Scliar's life was upended in 1964 by the coup d'état that overthrew President João Goulart, bringing in a military regime that lasted until 1985. This era was defined by political repression but also what came to be known as Brazil's "economic miracle." The military limited freedom in the name of national security, which Scliar understood as a call to arms for writers, who should use their storytelling talent to draw attention to government use of force. Throughout the decades, he explored that theme in multiple ways. A number of his characters are doctors, whose routine he analyses in detail, or else patients who undergo decisive medical procedures.

In the second half of the twentieth century, Brazil, like other Latin American countries, was swept by a new aesthetic movement, magical realism, in art, literature, film, and other genres. Capable of enchanting audiences while sidestepping censorship, in literature, the style juxtaposed modernity with dreamlike sequences, all presented in an unconventional baroque style. Writers such as Argentina's Julio Cortázar, Colombia's Gabriel García Márquez, Mexico's Carlos Fuentes, Chile's José Donoso, and Peru's Mario Vargas Llosa led the genre. They admired predecessors like Jorge Luis Borges and Juan Rulfo. In Brazil, the movement was represented by Jorge Amado, Nélida Piñon, Lygia Fagundes Telles, and João Ubaldo Ribeiro. They drew inspiration from Brazil's proto-modernist Joaquim Maria Machado de Assis, who used humor and innovative narrative devices to address pressing social questions.

The original term to describe the new aesthetic was *lo real maravilloso*, "that which is real and marvelous." It was coined by surrealism-influenced Cuban writer Alejo Carpentier after a trip to Haiti, where he recognized that surrealism, fashionable in Europe, existed in harmony with the environment in the Americas, in large part because the region fiercely resisted an embrace of modernity. Carpentier wrote about lo real maravilloso in the prologue to his novel *The Kingdom in This World* (1949). In retrospect, among the most vocal critique made of magical realism was its approach to Latin American society, which gave readers the impression that Latin America, by and large, was a universe where primitivism and Catholicism were interwoven. Probably that is why Scliar, celebrated as he was in Brazil since his early books, didn't fit the profile of authors initially selected for consumption by an international audience: He was Jewish.

As he made clear to me time and again, Scliar particularly loved the work of nineteenth-century Brazilian novelist Machado de Assis. He talked about other influences, especially depictions of Brazilian poverty in the *sertão*, the hinterland: Graciliano Ramos, author of *Barren Lives* (1938) and João Guimarães Rosa, known for *The Devil to Pay in the Backlands* (1956). But Scliar was defined by another tradition as well: European Jewish writers. Two enchanted him above all others: Franz Kafka and Isaac Babel. Like him, they wrote in non-Jewish languages, German and Russian, respectively. Scliar appreciated Kafka for his oblique critique of bureaucracy and the feeling of intense, almost uncontrollable anxiety that comes from being a modern Jew. In 1972, Scliar published the novel *The War of Bom Fim*. Mixing fantasy and realism, it follows Joel, who much like Scliar is a Jewish boy in the 1940s whose hero is Kafka.

Scliar was infatuated with Kafka's *The Metamorphosis* (1915), in which the protagonist, Gregor Samsa, wakes up from uneasy dreams to realize he has transformed into a huge insect. Scliar was especially fascinated by the transformation, which he stressed to me, isn't explicitly described. When the story begins, Gregor has already turned into a bug. As Kafka did, Scliar likewise explored angst and the Jewish body. His book *Kafka's Leopards* (2000), an overt tribute, is about Benjamin Kantarovich, a Trotskyite revolutionary in Russia in 1916—during "the ten days that shook the world"—who receives an encrypted message from Kafka about "leopards in the temple." One of Kafka's famously enigmatic aphorisms is "leopards break into the temple and drink all the sacrificial vessels dry; it keeps happening; in the end, it can be calculated in advance and is incorporated into the ritual." As the plot twists, Kantarovich ends up in Brazil during the 1964 coup d'état.

Scliar and I frequently talked about one particular story by Kafka that we both held in high esteem: "The Cares of a Family Man." The narrator, a family man, describes a bizarre creature called Odradek that lives in his house, is extraordinarily nimble, and can never be caught. This extract comes from Willa and Edwin Muir's translation:

> At first glance it looks like a flat star-shaped spool for thread, and indeed it does seem to have thread wound upon it; to be sure, they are only old,

broken-off bits of thread, knotted and tangled together, of the most varied sorts and colors. But it is not only a spool, for a small wooden crossbar sticks out of the middle of the star, and another small rod is joined to that at a right angle. By means of this latter rod on one side and one of the points of the star on the other, the whole thing can stand upright as if on two legs.

The Odradek "lurks by turns in the garret, the stairway, the lobbies, the entrance hall." He has humanoid qualities, including being able to speak: "'Well, what's your name?' you ask him. 'Odradek,' he says. 'And where do you live?' 'No fixed abode,' he says and laughs; but it is only the kind of laughter that has no lungs behind it. It sounds rather like the rustling of fallen leaves." This is the last paragraph of the story:

I ask myself, to no purpose, what is likely to happen to him? Can he possibly die? Anything that dies has had some kind of aim in life, some kind of activity, which has worn out; but that does not apply to Odradek. Am I to suppose, then, that he will always be rolling down the stairs, with ends of thread trailing after him, right before the feet of my children, and my children's children? He does no harm to anyone that one can see; but the idea that he is likely to survive me I find almost painful.

Written between 1914 and 1917, Kafka's story, as Scliar and I agreed, is a metaphor for Diasporism. The Odradek might be a monster, its existence amorphous, elusive, a threat, its future in doubt. Yet the family man, obsessed with this creature, talks about little else. There is a symbiotic relationship between the two, meaning that they depend on each other. In my own beguilement with the Odradek, I often imagine a counter-story, one narrated by the creature itself. How would the family man be depicted in it? And what kind of self-depiction would the Odradek offer about itself?

And then there is, with regard to Diasporism, my own favorite author: Sholom Aleichem. Scliar reminds me of him. Unlike Kafka and Babel, Sholom Aleichem wrote in a Jewish language: Yiddish. Scliar read Aleichem in Portuguese, particularly the novel *Tevye the Dairyman* (1895), which is the basis of *Fiddler on the Roof*. The humor of Sholom Aleichem, rooted in Ashkenazi life at the end of the nineteenth century, is realistic at its core: It explores poverty, assimilation, social mobility, immigration, and xenophobia. This, I am convinced, is where Scliar learned the power of humor.

SCLIAR'S BOOK OF J

A crucial diasporic novel by Scliar—and here, finally, I come to the volume you hold in your hand—is *The Woman Who Wrote the Bible* (1999), at last translated into English by Heath Wing. Most of the action takes place in King Solomon's temple in Jerusalem in the tenth century BCE. In spirit, though, it is clearly a narrative written from a perspective outside of Israel.

For you to appreciate the novel's scope, it is important that I explain its origins, at least in terms of my friendship with Scliar. It is well known in biblical scholarship that the Torah, as the Hebrew Bible is referred to among Jews, was canonized over a long period of time—more than a millennium—and was the product of a collection of disparate, anonymous authors with separate stylistic and ideological agendas. Of course, the rabbis behind the Babylonian Talmud argued that the Torah was written by God. Medieval thinkers like Maimonides, Hasdai Crescas, Solomon ibn Gabirol, and Yehuda Halevi held the same conviction. The Church Fathers agreed, too. However, this doesn't apply to the Apocrypha, and Protestants refute that scripture itself is divinely dictated.

Secularism endorsed the conception of the Bible as a human creation, and biblical scholarship is built around this notion. There are several identifiable authors of the Torah, each using a distinct term to refer to the divine, from Adonai (אֲדֹנָי) and Elohim (אֱלֹהִים), to Shaddai (שַׁדַּי), El (אֵל), Tzevaoth (צְבָאוֹת), and, most notably, the Tetragrammaton YHWH (יהוה), which, in its Latinized version, is variously spelled as Yaweh, Jehovah, or simply J.

The debate surrounding the divine names reached a crescendo, at least in the popular imagination, in 1990, when American poet David Rosenberg published a volume with a new English-language translation of only the segments in Genesis, Exodus, and Numbers attributed to J, which were composed between 950 and 900 BCE. No one had done so before. Rosenberg asked Harold Bloom, a Yale professor and critic whose keen interest in literature related to the Greek concept of *agon*, meaning "conflict," to write the book's introduction, which turned out to be rather explosive, making the book a cause célèbre and a *New York Times* bestseller. Bloom presented an explosive theory: Based on Rosenberg's translation, he argued that J wasn't a devout believer in God, as previous generations thought, but "a fierce ironist and a woman living in the court of King Solomon." In an age of political correctness, the idea that the biblical portions using "J" as God's appellation were handwritten by a female author delighted some and infuriated others. Feminists celebrated the thought but also argued it was implausible. Traditionalist readers attacked the thesis as another example of an anti-patriarchy rhetoric. Bloom took pleasure in the controversy because he himself had been an opponent of multiculturalism. In his introduction, Bloom claimed that the author of the biblical J ought to be compared to Homer, Shakespeare, and Tolstoy.

Almost as soon as it came out, Scliar and I both read *The Book of J*. Whenever we had an opportunity, we discussed it. What appealed to me, as I made clear to my friend, was Rosenberg's decision to use translation as a tool to selectively reintroduce discrete portions of the Torah. Translation, in my view, is never an innocent endeavor. While on the surface it seeks to transport a text from one linguistic habitat to another, its politics are often complicated. Why this particular text and not another? What agenda does the translator have, since no intellectual activity is ever disinterested? Rosenberg asked the reader to approach the portions written by J autonomously. What kind of author was J in terms of affinities, insouciances, and the like? Could we really talk of an author of the caliber of Homer or Shakespeare, for instance? Granted, Homer and Shakespeare are themselves challenging, since biographically we know next to nothing about the first, whereas the second is the source of a long-lasting school of skeptics known as the non-Stratfordians. Still, is it truly possible to talk about J as an individual? And, more intriguingly, can we talk about J as a woman, at a time when women were excluded from the intellectual elite? Needless to say, in *The Five Books of Moses* men are dominant in countless ways, starting with Genesis 2:21–24, in the King James Bible:

> And the Lord God caused a deep sleep to fall upon Adam, and he slept; and he took one of his ribs, and closed up the flesh instead thereof; And the rib, which the LORD God had taken from man, made he a woman, and brought her unto the man. And Adam said, "This *is* now bone of my bones, and flesh of my flesh: she shall be called Woman, because she was taken out of Man.

Therefore shall a man leave his father and his mother, and shall cleave unto his wife: and they shall be one flesh."

Following this are the numerous sections on the matriarchs Sarah, Rachel, Leah, and Rebecca. Might there be a hidden, subterranean message in this dichotomy?

In contrast, reading the *Book of J* evoked in Scliar a sublime magical moment, perhaps the best he ever had. He wrote to me that, while in biblical scholarship Bloom's hypothesis might not be taken seriously, it was extraordinarily juicy for a novelist like him. What kind of woman in King Solomon's harem could have come up with such a mythopoetic narrative? A few months later, in 1998, he sent me the manuscript. And a year later, I got an early copy, in Portuguese, of *A Mulher que escreveu a Biblia*.

The result is thrilling. Concretely, he isn't interested in describing Jerusalem, the capital of the Israelite kingdom, with any dose of nostalgia. Although the reader follows the female protagonist as she moves from her father's home to the palace, the landscape is barely described. Nor do we reach the point, a few centuries later, in circa 587 BCE, when Israel collapses as a kingdom as Nebuzaradan, the captain of the guard of King Nebuchadnezzar of Babylon, burns the Jewish temple in Jerusalem, an episode described in the Bible in 2 Kings 25.9–10. Instead, Scliar delves into the interior life of the female narrator, who is one of King Solomon's legendary seven hundred wives and three hundred concubines. He does it by ridiculing sexual abuse at the palace. As such, *The Woman Who Wrote the Bible* is a feminist critique.

The novel opens in an unspecified Brazilian location that could be Porto Alegre. The bulk of the plot takes place in Jerusalem, mostly in King Solomon's palace. In quick succession two narrators, one male, the other female, take command: one is an ex-historian who becomes a therapist of past lives and has a crush on a patient, told in a first-person account. The second is the patient, whose letter about a past life in part—just in part—explains the relationship between them. The novel juxtaposes high biblical diction with raunchy aestheticism.

From the start, Scliar seems to advise the reader to be cautious. Don't take this too seriously. It is a game! Yet his midrash—a Hebrew term denoting an interpretation that looks at a text from all possible standpoints, including the letters in which it is delivered—goes deep into the connection between wisdom and sexuality. His King Solomon is an instinctual jurist whose knowledge, as legend goes, doesn't come from books but from speaking to birds, including doves, swallows, and peacocks. He is also a fraud. In spite of his reputation as an inexhaustible lover in a pre-Viagra age, his public persona doesn't quite match the flaccid organ revealed in his private chambers. Might it be because that wife is ugly—"repressively ugly," "furiously ugly," "modestly ugly or proudly so," "satisfyingly ugly," "ugly, always ugly"? Or could his inadequate performance be proof of undiagnosed erectile dysfunction?

In a country like Brazil where plastic surgery is an obsession, describing the female protagonist as ugly and the king as sexually tame isn't blasphemous. More than anything else, the woman who writes Scliar's Bible is a savvy Scheherazade.

After devouring the novel, I sent Scliar a congratulatory email on his rewriting of *The Book of J*, telling him his unique touch was palpable on every page. The bureaucratic dealings the woman author of the Torah faces in the palace of King Solomon felt Kafkaesque. Other sections reminded me of *A majestade do Xingu* in its embrace of a rebel who becomes a keeper of communal memory. And I saw traces of Guedali Tartakovsky, the protagonist of *The Centaur in the Garden*, who navigates a hostile environment by reinventing himself, becoming an impostor. Impostors, Scliar proposes, are daring, nonconformist creators.

Obviously, Scliar's takeoff of *The Book of J* isn't a theological treatise. Nor is it a religious text. In fact, his novel is only tangentially about the Bible. Instead, it is about its scaffoldings. In the hands of such a superb storyteller, the mere possibility that a woman is behind key portions of the Torah is an exquisite invitation to rethink the book many people have rigid, fixed ideas about. Oscar Wilde, in his play *The Importance of Being Earnest* (1895), posits that "the truth is rarely pure and never simple." He suggests that to open a book without an open mind is a contradiction in terms. Scliar proves him right.

In my note to Scliar, I added that, as far as I knew, this was the first time a Latin American Jewish author dared to place a plotline in ancient Jerusalem. "Obligado," he responded immediately, adding that art allows us to return to crucial historical epochs, although never in a neutral way. It reinvents those periods. Fiction set in the past is not about what happened but what we imagine happened. He argued that truth in science and truth in literature are different: whereas in the former, one must stick to the facts, the other is open to rearrangement. Yet through those rearrangements it touches sacred truths impossible to ignore.

Sometime later, Scliar wrote me to say that *The Woman Who Wrote the Bible* received the Jabuti Award, Brazil's most prestigious literary prize. We reminisced about the circuitous topics we explored during our travels: from Maimonides and Machado de Assis to Sholom Aleichem, Kafka, and Philip Roth. I told him that in my eyes his oeuvre, like Stefan Zweig's, was a response to destructive ideologies. Through levity and incisive intellectual engagement, he proved yet again that the Jewish diaspora, while defined by conflict, is a machine of endless creativity.

TRANSLATOR'S NOTE

Originally published in 1999, Moacyr Scliar's *The Woman Who Wrote the Bible* speculates that the Jahwist source of the Hebrew Bible was actually a woman. Often abbreviated as J, the Jahwist source is identified in what is known as the documentary hypothesis—a model developed by biblical scholars to explain the composition of the Torah. (This model has since fallen out of favor.) That J was a woman was originally posited by Harold Bloom in *The Book of J* (1990). Inspired by Bloom's highly speculative thesis, Scliar went on to adapt and expand on its premise in his novel.

The Woman Who Wrote the Bible poses the question: In the hyper-patriarchal world of the Middle East in the tenth century BCE, under what circumstances would a woman learn to read and write, much less be commissioned to write what would become one of the most important texts in human history? The answers to this line of inquiry provide the point of departure for the novel's narrative, which mercilessly pokes fun at the absurdities of patriarchy and the commodification of feminine beauty. Following the biblical tradition of women like Esther, Tamar, and Deborah, Scliar ultimately imagines a woman who, despite the limitations that her world places on her, manipulates the status quo to achieve her own self-interests.

In some ways, Scliar's novel recalls Joseph Heller's *God Knows* (1985). Both Scliar and Heller were brilliant satirists, and both *The Woman Who Wrote the Bible* and *God Knows* re-create biblical narratives with voices that sound modern. Yet, where Heller's novel narrates the life of King David from David's point of view, Scliar's relies on the first-person narrative of a provincial woman who is sent to live in King Solomon's harem. Scliar therefore retrofits his main character into the story of King Solomon from the Bible. This affords him a unique perspective through which he can subvert established biblical lore that lionizes the ancient patriarch, such as legendary accounts of King Solomon's wisdom.

Unlike Joseph Heller's *God Knows*, Scliar employs a clever plot device that accounts for his novel's use of modern anachronisms: His narrator is actually a contemporary woman who, after completing several sessions with her "past-life therapist," becomes convinced that she once lived in the tenth century BCE, as one of King Solomon's seven hundred wives. This discovery leads her to write down the story of her past life, revealing not only how she came to be one of King Solomon's many wives, but also how she came to write the Bible. The novel's re-creation of ancient Israel, presented through the first-person narrative of a woman whose voice is modern in tone, produces a unique reading experience that is at once hilarious and thought-provoking. Although set in ancient Israel, the novel speaks to the contemporary sociocultural milieu of Brazil and of the modern world in general.

Several years ago, a friend brought to my attention the fact that *The Woman Who Wrote the Bible* had never been translated into English. A scholar of religious studies, he came across mention of the novel in an article. When he asked me if I had heard of it, I confirmed that I had, and that I was a fan of the author in general, but that I had not read it. His response was along the lines of, "Well, someone needs to translate it into English so I can read it." This short conversation left me curious. When I read the novel not long after, its humorous use of language—the blending of Brazilian slang with dated biblical lexicon and verse—had me smiling to myself immediately. It was a translator's dream. I knew I wanted to translate it, and I was soon fortunate to find myself taking on the project.

When I translated the novel, preserving its humor was my number-one priority. Often my decisions hinged on whether I thought my rendering was funny. Friends served as my sounding board. They got used to me asking them random questions like, "Does Daddy-God or Pappa-God sound funnier?" This was also true of my approach to the book's vulgarity. My partner got sick of me asking her which phallic descriptor or verb for copulation she preferred in a certain context. "Does it matter?" she finally asked. "Of course it does!" I responded, my hair disheveled, my eyes bloodshot, like a mad scientist on the verge of a breakthrough. "If it doesn't matter, then what am I doing? If it doesn't matter, all of humanity is lost!" I must include that she was adamant about one thing: that I use the word *stone* instead of *rock*, because a stone is smooth and a rock is not. You will understand why this matters once you delve into the book. That I ever used *rock* is massively embarrassing on my part.

While my approach may sound a bit dramatic, I was motivated by the reality that humor can be a challenge to translate across cultures. A joke that doesn't land just doesn't land, regardless of how good it is in the original language. The biblical setting of the novel did make translating the book's humor easier, given that the Bible is a shared touchstone in Western cultures. Moreover, I quickly learned that the best approach was to lean into the humor instead of shying away from it. So I leaned into the mix of archaic and modern language. And I leaned into the idea of what I could discover in translation, instead of fearing what would be lost in translation (a cliché I despise). For instance, when confronted with a passage where the protagonist is attempting to seduce King Solomon with her writing, instead of a verbatim translation rendered as "My hopes of seducing Solomon via parchment were sunk," I went with "My hopes of sexting Solomon via parchment were sunk." The convenience of a contemporary word in English that literally means "to seduce or have sex through text" was too good to pass up. Sexting also juxtaposes nicely with the antiquated technology of writing on parchment. Plus, had I not used sexting, surely some attentive reader would have noticed my missed opportunity, shrugged, and called me a hack.

I also discovered Yiddish—well, not literally. I am not the Christopher Columbus of Yiddish. I do not claim to be the first person to discover a language that millions have spoken and speak. I also do not mean that Scliar employed Yiddish in his novel. No, what I mean is that Yiddish just kind of crept into my translation. Maybe it was due to growing up on Mel Brooks movies or *Seinfeld*, but I couldn't help but identify Scliar's humor with that of Jewish American comedians. Here, however, I was careful. I did not lean in but kept that influence to a minimum. Less was more. It became a nod to Scliar's Yiddish-speaking heritage, to the Yiddish-speaking household he grew up in. Scliar, who grew up in the faraway land of Rio Grande do Sul, wrote in a language, Brazilian Portuguese, that does not have Yiddish loanwords in its everyday vernacular. American English, in contrast, has borrowed many Yiddish words. Even I, a hick who grew up in a small town in a faraway land called West Texas, far from any Jewish community, grew up with a few Yiddish words peppered in my vocabulary. Words that as a kid I didn't even know were Yiddish. They were just words. Like *putz*, which I believe entered usage in our household via *Grumpy Old Men*. My dad loved the movie, and he laughed every time Walter Matthau called Jack Lemmon a putz.

During the translation process, what I would or would not allow was determined by the novel's inner logic and linguistic world. So I allowed *sexting* because the book consistently included anachronisms and wordplay in other places. Or I justified the usage of a few Yiddish words because Scliar employed words from other modern languages in the novel, like French. As the novel's primary funny bone, the varying linguistic registers were the focus of my translation, and I made sure to accentuate their contrasts.

The Woman Who Wrote the Bible is probably Scliar's most irreverent, humorous novel. And although his many works vary in tone, he always made room for some form of humor. He even wrote about humor, especially about Jewish humor within the broader context of Jewish identity and history. In one of his crónicas (newspaper columns), titled "From Eden to the Couch: Jewish Humor," he reflects:

> All cultures utilize humor to some degree or another. Judaism certainly does. With one particularity: for Jews, humor is more than a way to tell stories; it is a way of life, of survival, even. In Jewish history, marked by exile, by persecution, by massacre, humor emerges as a defense, at times the only defense, against desperation. That is why it is a bitter, melancholic humor that makes you smile, not laugh. It is a philosophical humor that makes you think.

Scliar's sense of humor certainly checks the abovementioned boxes. It can be bitter, melancholic, and philosophical. It can certainly make you smile and make you think. But, I would add, it can also make you laugh.

Scliar specifically addresses the Jewish comedic tradition in the United States as well. On this topic, he cites the Brazilian humorist Luis Fernando Verissimo, a good friend of his: "In the United States, out of every ten comedians, nine are Jews and one isn't very good." Scliar clearly got a kick out his friend's comment. And he certainly admired his friend's sense of humor, just as Verissimo admired his friend's literary achievements, once stating that he considered Scliar to be "one of the great Brazilian writers." I would suggest that Scliar is one of the greats not just because of his fine storytelling, but because he is so darned funny. I think Verissimo would agree. Melancholically funny, bitterly funny, absurdly funny or philosophically funny, always funny.

HEATH WING

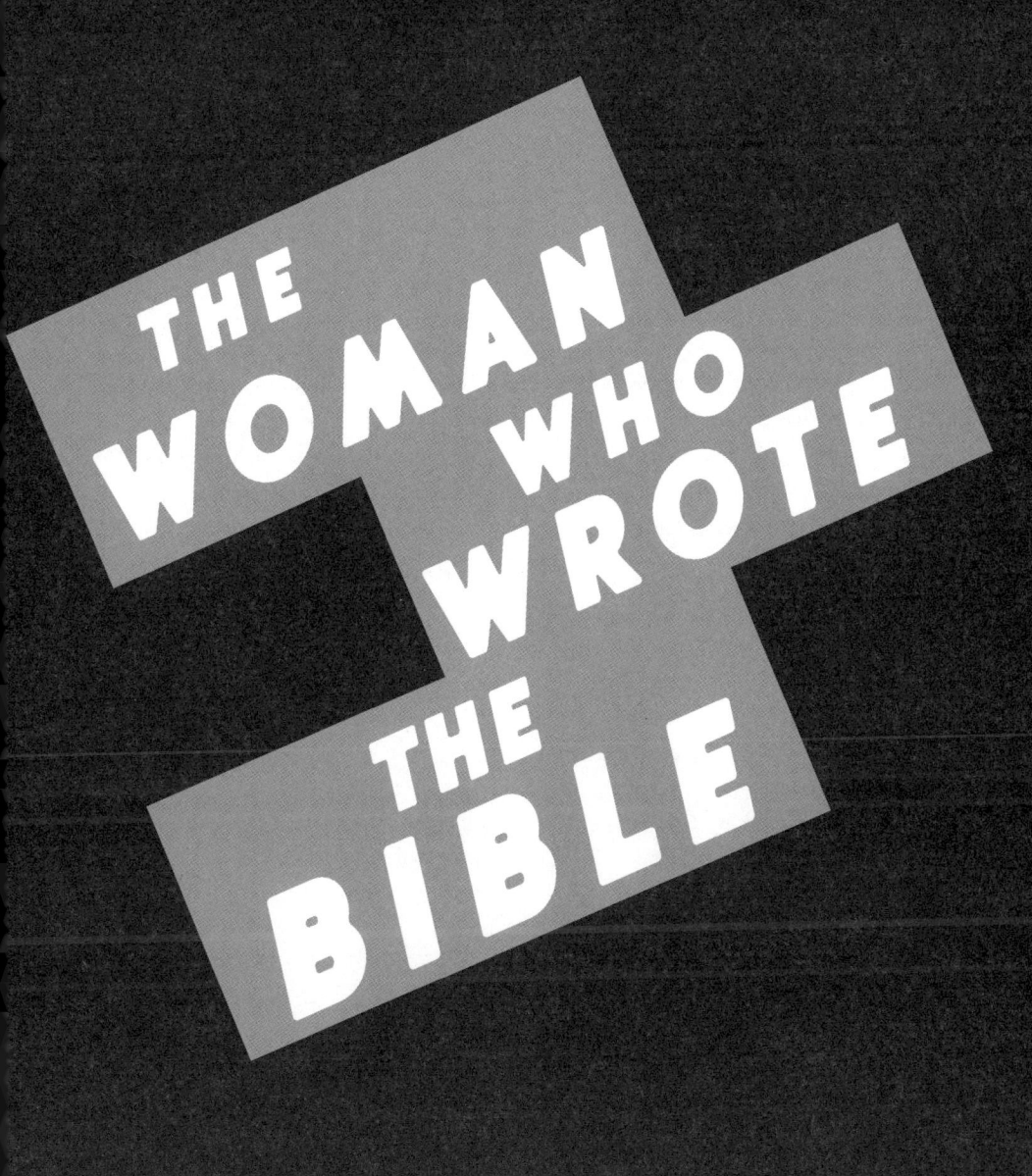

In Jerusalem, nearly three thousand years ago, an unknown author [J] composed a work that has formed the spiritual consciousness of much of the world ever since. ...J was not a professional scribe but rather an immensely sophisticated, highly placed member of the Solomonic elite, enlightened and ironic...a woman, who wrote for her contemporaries as a woman.

—HAROLD BLOOM, *THE BOOK OF J*

MANY PEOPLE ASK ME why I work in past-life therapy. My answer varies depending on the circumstances. When interviewed on TV or the radio—and I'm often interviewed—I state, in an intentionally reticent sort of way, that fate brought me to my line of work. The result is generally pretty good, eliciting exclamations of awe from interviewers and any audience that may be present. Fate is a word that people really like; they associate it with the supernatural, with the alignment of stars, things that instill a sense of wonder. Taking advantage of this tingling sensation, I press on. At first with intentional difficulty—hesitant pauses, painful silences—but then with growing enthusiasm, as if the floodgates had opened—you know, the floodgates of emotion. I make it known that I was originally a history teacher. Which, again, is a surprise: everyone usually imagines psychologist or doctor.

I don't share how I landed on history, mostly because it's of no interest to the public, and even if it were, I still wouldn't explain myself. But it was my father, the old commie Aurélio Silva, who encouraged it. A blue-collar worker, what he earned in printmaking made for a bad living, what with a wife and five kids to support. But he had unshakable faith in the future, synthesized into what was for him a single magic word: Communism. There never was, and there never will be, anyone else with such belief in an ideal. He was not simply a militant but a studious devotee of the doctrine. He used to devour each and every book his comrades loaned him. Since he had little time to spare, he would read into unholy hours of the night, despite my mother's protests. The next day at work was always a struggle. Exhausted, he would often nod off, which eventually resulted in a tragic accident: the paper cutter he was operating lopped off his right hand. Maimed, he was summarily let go. His comrades from the Party arranged another job for him—union watchman—but his life was never the same. He would easily fall into despair and burst out crying for no reason. My mother didn't know what to do. My siblings had little patience. It was up to me, then, to give him some measure of support. We used to converse for hours on end. Converse, no, he would talk and I would listen. And he always talked about his militant past. "The works of Marx," he used to say, eyes welling up, "were for me a revelation." Truth be told, he had only read a summary of Das Capital, but that was all it took for the light bulb to go off in his head: history had meaning; more than that, it had laws.

Was it because of our conversations that I chose history? I think so. You see, it was as if I were compensating him for his lost hand and for his suffering... He cried for joy when I passed my college entrance exams. "You will be what I couldn't be," he used to say, "a great intellectual, a leader of the Party."

Who was he kidding, the poor man! I was a lefty, but no militant. I never toed the Party line. In college I participated in a few protest movements; I attended marches, distributed pamphlets, but when I finished school I stopped being interested in politics. I had a diploma and I needed to earn a living—at that point my father had died, and supporting my mother was the only thing on my mind, because I lived with her. I liked teaching, so I got a job as a teacher at a public high school. The salary was bad, the school poor and limited in resources, but what mostly rubbed me wrong was the fact that the students couldn't have cared less. "Why do we have to learn about the Egyptians and their pharaohs?" they would ask. "Those dudes died a long time ago." My students were little shits, and I was on the verge of blowing a fuse and sending them all to hell. Before leaving the high school, however, I decided to give it one last try. I came up with a game where each student had to role-play a historical figure. To my surprise, it was a hit with the kids. It generated buzz at school: kings, counts, generals were all the students talked about. The other teachers, impressed, complimented me on the idea.

And then it happened.

One of the students, a very quiet boy of humble extraction, decided to play the part of some prince or other, I don't remember which. He totally went method for his role. He spent hours in the library researching the life of his character until the librarian actually had to send him away. His behavior changed; he treated his classmates in a strange, aggressive way. Many of them complained, but I didn't pay them much heed. After all, he was just a teenager, and teenagers are weird.

It was the kid's mom. "What did you do to my son, Mister?" she shouted as soon as she saw me. I tried to calm her down, asked her to tell me what was going on. Visibly annoyed, she said her son wouldn't listen to her anymore. He had become arrogant, a bully. He would no longer make his bed, would leave his clothes scattered on the floor for someone else to pick up.

"It's your fault," she complained. "All because of that stupid game you made up."

She wanted to file a complaint with the school board, but I managed to dissuade her. "I'll take care of it," I promised.

I called the kid in for a private chat. Undeniably, he was no longer the same Luizinho who used to speak to me with his head down, eyes on the floor. What I had before me now was someone with princely posture. I carefully asked if he had noticed the change and what he attributed it to. At first he answered with arrogance—he didn't owe me an explanation, who was I but a two-bit teacher—but then, suddenly, the waters parted. Yes, something had happened, something extraordinary. He wasn't just playing a part; he was living another existence entirely. He had gone back to the past, and in doing so, had discovered that in reality he wasn't a prince, as he had modestly supposed, but a king, a powerful and cruel monarch, of the kind who doesn't hesitate to order the slaughter of their enemies. "I already liquidated more than three thousand," he confirmed proudly. He told me in great detail about one of the executions, carried out in the large courtyard of the royal castle, with a large crowd in attendance. He described to me how the executioner positioned the neck of the condemned on the stump, how he decapitated him with one swing of his axe, blood spraying all over people in the front row. I must say, I was impressed. It was as if the kid had lived the whole thing. Upon finishing his narrative, he sincerely thanked me for giving him the chance to go back in time and find his true self.

"You shall be rewarded," he promised, and walked off.

Bewildered, I didn't know what to think. But I soon recognized the extraordinary possibilities that the kid's case afforded me. A new door opened to me: I would become a past-life therapist.

That's the story I tell in interviews. And I've told it so many times that it has become truth for me. Fact or fiction, what's true is that people like it, and that's what matters. Soon after, I quite naturally took a course on past-life therapy, but the method I use is my own, based on the knowledge I gained as a history teacher. My patients go back in time, and as soon as their visions start, I explain: "That place where you are is the royal palace, that man in armor facing you is Frederick the Great, those others are courtiers..." I like to say I play the role of a guide, leading people through the twists and turns of time.

Success came immediately. I began to treat people in a small office of an old building downtown. Word soon got out. Demand skyrocketed, profits followed. I had to find a bigger and more comfortable place—more appropriate for the premium clientele I now had. A real estate agent helped me find an old house on a quiet street in the suburbs. I went there, and no sooner had I walked in than I knew it was the perfect place: The stairway at the entrance garrisoned by lions, the spacious rooms, hardwood wainscoting, Portuguese tiles in the hallways, antique lighting fixtures, everything recalled the past. It was undoubtedly the ideal setting for people wanting to turn back the hands of time. With my success already consolidated, the move was the cherry on top. I was pursued by business magnates, artists, TV actors. I moved into a new apartment, bought an imported car. I enjoyed the media coverage. Self-help publishers harassed me to write a book.

It was then that she walked through my doors.

One afternoon, my secretary informed me that someone wanted to see me, a young woman who had seen me on TV and come to the conclusion that past-life therapy was exactly what she needed.

"She's the daughter of a large landowner," added my secretary with a wink. In other words, the girl had cash to burn, which wasn't a must, of course, but it didn't hurt either. I took her on, admitted her for treatment.

In the first session she cried a lot. Told me she didn't get along well with her father: He doesn't understand me, never understood me, was never able to get close to me—a tale as old as time. According to her, except for one sister who was her confidant, she lived alone in her own little fantasy world. She consoled herself with books, reading and studying constantly. She attended a school run by nuns and was considered one of the best students there. She had won several awards for her knowledge of the Bible. For example, she knew the Song of Songs by heart.

About a year ago she had lived through a painful ordeal, something that changed her life. She fell in love with a farmhand, a good-looking fellow, but odd and aloof. One minor detail: They had lived in each other's orbit since childhood, but always at a distance until suddenly it happened, that abrupt, inexplicable break. She couldn't get him out of her head. She had eyes only for him, wanting only to be with him. And then came the doubt. Should she tell him about her feelings? Unlike other guys, he seemed to look at her kindly, with affection even. She mustered her courage and decided to open up and tell him everything. But on the day she was going to do it, a scandal broke out in her family: a love affair involving the sister. The young farmhand had taken her virginity. Furious, the landowner had the little miscreant beaten and then kicked him off his land.

She couldn't share her sense of betrayal with anyone. Such was her suffering that she resolved to leave the small town where she lived and come to the big city. She got a job at a large company. The work wasn't all that bad and people at the office treated her well, but she couldn't get over what had happened. On the contrary, she felt increasingly worse. She became depressed, slept poorly.

An interview I gave on TV was—in her words—a real revelation. In past-life therapy she would find the solution to her problems. She said that she was certain I could help guide her through the labyrinth of the past where the answer to her troubles lay hidden. Her eagerness was apparent, but I was on the fence. Something told me I wouldn't be just taking on another patient. I was entering a minefield. At any rate, we began sessions regardless, and soon she was traveling back in time. Her visions brought her to a palace she had seen in her dreams, which turned out to be King Solomon's palace (which, by the way, was a problem for me—I knew very little about the Bible and had to study to keep up). There, she was one of the many wives of the monarch, whom she described as a handsome and charming man. She was profoundly in love with him. True, her love was unrequited, but that didn't keep her from fantasizing scenes of hot sex in Solomon's bed—scenes that she described in titillating detail.

Before long I found out that behind it all was a hidden purpose: she was in love with me, and such descriptions were directed at me. Once, she even tried to hug me. Delicately but firmly, I stopped her, explaining that it would be a mistake, that she was confusing the present with the past. A love affair with a patient would be too risky for me. It was the last thing I wanted.

But that wasn't the problem. The problem was that her stories shook me. More than once I caught myself eyeing her breasts through her half-open blouse. Petite, beautiful breasts, two harmonious exaltations. Through the valley of those breasts I wanted to walk; I wanted to climb them, lick their nipples . . . which left me rather alarmed, confused. She, as incredible as it may seem, was oblivious. She had accepted my rejection. What's more, her energy was now spent on seducing her beloved Solomon. I didn't have the nerve to tell her, "Stop yanking my dick, you're here and so am I. What matters is the present. If you want to make love, let's get it on right here and right now." After each session she would cordially say goodbye and leave, without anything happening. And me? I would lock myself in the bathroom and masturbate. Like a horny teenager.

My anxiety only grew worse when my secretary told me a man had picked her up from the clinic after waiting around for her. From the description she gave, I had no doubt in my mind it was her dad's former employee, obviously eager to correct his mistake and sleep with the right daughter. Which was far from good news. Between King Solomon and her new lover my chances were slim. I needed to speed things up. I wasn't just up against time travel, I was in a race against the clock. My torment haunted me in my dreams. In them I was Solomon, except the woman in my bed was not my patient but the Queen of Sheba, who had traveled a great distance to visit me and to whom I was to give political and sexual counsel. In other words, I was screwing one woman while thinking about another.

I would wake up from those dreams drenched in sweat. I decided I had to confess my love to her. Immediately. This whole business of past-life therapy was going to be the end of me. Nonetheless, how to do it? How could I backtrack after rejecting her?

One morning she called my secretary to let her know that she wouldn't be coming in for therapy. She left a note, however, asking me to stop by her apartment later that afternoon. A surprise was waiting for me there.

A surprise? My God, what surprise could it be? What would I find when the door of destiny opened? Would she be there in a black negligee, her beautiful breasts quivering for me? Had our big moment finally arrived?

Time stood still that afternoon. My patients droned on and on. One woman was decapitated during the French Revolution, some man sailed the seven seas in a caravel, another elderly woman fought in the American Civil War—I wasn't paying attention. I kept checking my watch. By four in the afternoon I couldn't take it anymore. I told my secretary to cancel my remaining appointments and ran to her apartment, which was several blocks away. When I rounded the corner, my heart almost stopped.

She was exiting the apartment building with her arms around a man, the two laughing happily. I didn't know the guy, but I didn't doubt for a second that he was her dad's former employee. He carried a suitcase, hers presumably. They got in a taxi and left.

I went into the building and took the elevator up to the apartment she shared with a coworker. That's who answered the door. She asked if I was the therapist and, after I confirmed I was, said she had something for me. "It's from your former patient," she said. "She's gone and won't be coming back, but she left this here."

She gave me a letter and a binder. The letter, written in a hurry, said goodbye and thank you. My sage advice had led her to a somewhat surprising outcome. The anger she felt toward the guy who had swapped her out for her sister was no more, and in its place had blossomed renewed love. He was her king, the monarch she had dreamed of.

As for the binder, it contained a story she had written based on her travels to the past. She dedicated it to me; I was authorized to do as I pleased with the narrative. I could even publish it as long as I didn't mention her name.

That's the story I've read day and night since she left. I look for myself in her story. I search for myself in the text, between the lines, in proper and common names;

I search for myself among verbs and adverbs, in the periods, the commas, the ellipses. And I don't find me. I fail to find myself anywhere. I am lost.

I continue to treat people at my clinic, but I've given serious thought to changing course and taking up history again. I'll earn less, live less lavishly, but I hope I can pick up the pieces. I want to forget her.

What else? Oh yes, she was ugly.

UGLINESS IS KEY, AT least for understanding this story. The one doing the talking, she's ugly. Very ugly. She's repressively ugly or furiously ugly, shamefully ugly or openly ugly, modestly ugly or proudly so, sad ugly or happy ugly, frustratingly ugly or satisfyingly ugly—but ugly, always ugly.

I'd suspected it ever since childhood, that I was ugly. The other girls in the village, pretty in general, were reluctant to play with me; whenever I showed my face, they would find a way to sneak off, giggling. Now, I was neither lame nor stupid, so why did they flee? It was something they saw in me and refused to address. So, as unbelievable as it may seem, I would only discover the extent of my ugliness at the ripe old age of eighteen. My coconspirator in all this, ironically, was my younger sister, my friend and confidant I turned to whenever I needed to talk about something.

One afternoon, I went into our room, and there she was. Assuming herself alone, she sat looking in a mirror.

I didn't know my sister had a mirror. Nobody knew my sister had a mirror. What's more, no one knew there was a mirror in the house. In the first place, a mirror was expensive; only nobles and rich landowners could afford one. This was not the case with our father. Even though he was the patriarch of our village, he barely owned one herd of goats, and it wasn't the biggest herd out there. Actually, back in my grandfather's day our people had been nomads, living in tents, wandering the desert in search of grazing for our goats. It had always been that way and everything indicated it would always be so. My father, however, decided our tribe should have a fixed residence. His dream was for us to form a city center, a city that would quicky grow and become a metropolis, perhaps the capital of an empire. He was an ambitious and ornery man, albeit not very bright. And surly: He couldn't stand being challenged. When someone would ask him about his coming metropolis, about his empire, he restrained himself by answering dryly: "You'll see."

And he said nothing more.

Meanwhile, as my father's prophesized future refused to arrive, we continued living in a small, austere house. Limited furniture, zero comforts; anything that hinted of luxury was an abomination. So even if he could have bought a mirror, he wouldn't have. "Such things are demonic," he would say, "behind every mirror lurks the Evil One, ready to deploy vanity to seduce people into sin." Not that he was an example of high morals. He was a known womanizer, the type who covets his neighbor's wife. On top of that, he was mixed up in some shady business—part of his herd was, to use a euphemism, of dubious origin. But that didn't stop him from posing as the morality police. He demanded irreproachable behavior from his tribe, and especially from his family. He was intolerant of the slightest manifestation of vanity in his daughters.

My sister was eager to disobey my father's will as soon as she obtained a small round mirror (how, I would only discover later), the mirror she was now gazing into. Enthralled, and with good reason. She was pretty. As pretty as I was ugly. Large eyes, delicate nose, full lips... Pretty but imprudent: She'd forgotten the door was open. That's how I was able to catch her in the act of full-on transgression.

She jumped when she saw me and tried to hide the mirror. Before she could do so, I grabbed for it. "Give me that!" I shouted furiously, "I want to take a look at myself too." She immediately recognized the danger I was in and tried to dissuade me: "Don't do it! This mirror is cursed. It bewitched me and it'll bewitch you too. Our father was right to prohibit such a demonic thing. Don't look at yourself, please; don't look at yourself. It's vanity, an abomination. I already sinned, don't you sin too."

Her pleas and desperation profited nothing. Deep down I knew she wanted to spare me from something that for me was still unknown: the devastating revelation of my ugliness, which up to that point I'd only suspected. Having seen the mirror, however, I wasn't about to back down for anything in the world. The temptation was irresistible, like gravity's pull, so to speak. Well, let gravity take me, what did I care? In search of the truth, I would willingly take the plunge. Deep down, maybe I was hoping for a miracle, that the mirror would show me a surprisingly lovely face, or at least one not completely ugly. Perhaps it was a magic mirror, magic only for me, mind you, not for anyone else; a mirror able to get in touch with a person's deepest desires and channel psychic energy that would instantly curate a complete reordering and embellishment of facial lines—that whole frog-turning-into-a-prince schtick. What I thought, what I craved in that instant, I fail to remember. All I know is that I wanted the mirror and would do anything to get it.

Panicking, my sister tried to flee. I was quick on her heels and tackled her. We fought. Only a little. She was no match for me. What I lacked in beauty I made up for in strength. I subdued her, took the mirror out of her hand. And that was that; now it was mine.

It wasn't the best of mirrors: a simple bronze disc, polished, of poor quality. But it did what all mirrors are supposed to do, for the well-being or disgrace of those who look in them. It showed a face. My face.

I couldn't believe what I was seeing. My God, is that me in there?

There was no symmetry in that face, much less the fearful symmetry of the tiger's muzzle. I searched in vain for some sort of harmony. I wasn't asking for some great spherical perfection, just a little sex appeal would have been nice, but I didn't even get that. My face was overloaded with conflict, the mouth out of tune with the nose, the ears out of tune with each other. And the eyes, which could have saved the whole thing, were cross-eyed, one of them uncomfortably gazing into the mirror, the other with a lost look, staring forsakenly into the distance, perhaps to avoid taking in my cruel reflection. Details (but must I go into details? Yes, I must spill the deets, dive deep into the pit of despair): moles. Spread all over my face, I had—I didn't count, but I think two dozen is a conservative estimate—moles. Moles galore, a preposterous collection of moles, an out-of-control outbreak of moles. The sheer assortment could constitute the subject matter of a treatise on dermatology. They varied in size and shape. One of them in particular made me squeamish. Such a protrusion, it almost dangled there, balancing helplessly in the air. Strong winds were not uncommon in our region, and all it would take would be a strong wind to untether it and carry it off. If it fell among rocks it would wither and die, if it fell on desert sands it would wither and die, if it fell into the crater of a volcano it would wither and die—and upon its withering and dying I would rejoice. But if it fell on fertile ground . . . if it fell on fertile ground it would germinate, and God only knows what plant would sprout forth, what bizarre tree with gnarly and parched branches. Even if the specimen were intuitively given the epithet Ugly-Girl Tree, I would stage no protest. At best, I could try to chop it down in the dead of night.

In summary, this is what I saw: (a) flagrant asymmetry; (b) lack of harmony; (c) cross-eyedness (albeit moderate); (d) moles in excess. It should be said that this was all framed (framed! That's a good one, framed! Like a pretty painting is framed! Framed I tell you!) by a dry, matted head of hair, capable of bringing any hairdresser to their knees.

What the mirror showed me was something resembling a strange, tormented landscape where geographical mishaps (mishaps: a very appropriate term) hadn't the slightest relationship with each other. A catastrophe had taken place on my face, a cataclysm that surely had long preceded my birth. What I was seeing was archaic ugliness, ugliness ancestral, accumulated over the years, over millennia, perhaps.

Face in her hands, my sister sobbed quietly. I didn't feel bad seeing her like that. On the contrary, what I felt was anger—immense, savage anger—at her, at my other sister, at my parents. Why hadn't they told me before that I was so ugly? Why had they deceived me?

The most obvious answer was pity. They had tried to spare me the overwhelming reality through painstaking collusion. Throughout the years, they had been characters in a comedy, successfully staged for a limited audience: me. "Here she comes! Quick, pretend we don't notice her face, pretend she's normal, a little attractive, even—don't act astonished by her beauty because that's a hard sell; too much alms and the saint will be suspicious, just act natural and it will land right." I, the lone spectator, was easily fooled. In reality, their performance, now that I was forced to see the truth, was superb. Nobody spoke of my features; nobody said, for example, You're so pretty—but also no one said, You're so hideous. They kept their mouths shut, or they tiptoed through the daisies of a compliment: You look as pretty as that frock. The affirmative "you look pretty" was always accompanied by a relativizing complement ("as that frock"), which would soften the lie, making it tolerable in the eyes of Jehovah while at the same time propping up the merciful illusion.

It would have taken only an ounce of attention to know it was all a sham. But had I wanted to detect the sham? Or had I participated in it, fooling myself, on the one hand, to not thwart my improv troupe of a family, and on the other, to evade the terrifying truth?

My misgivings no longer added up. The farce no longer held. Confronted with reality, I couldn't escape it. Oh, if I could only go back . . . Why did I look at myself in that mirror, I wondered, beating my chest with unrestrained fury, why did I give in to my accursed curiosity? Damn my vanity. Why didn't Jehovah rip that eye-opening yet sinister object from my hands? Huh, Jehovah? Why didn't you take action, all-powerful Mr. Know-It-All? You could have reduced the mirror to dust by your word alone. Why didn't you do it? Could it be that you don't exist, amigo? Huh? Could it be that you're nothing but an abstraction, an emotionally charged optical illusion?

Outcry and recrimination were of no use. Nothing more could be done. I had looked at myself in the mirror, and that was all she wrote. I would never forget what I had seen. But I needed, if not consolation, at least an explanation. I had to know the reason behind my outsized portion of ugliness. Nature couldn't have acted alone in the construction of my face. Undoubtedly it was the penalty for some sin or crime. But what sin, what crime had I committed? In search of an answer, I revisited my childhood. True, I was mean, but no more so than your average kid. I used to hit my sisters, but only occasionally, and even then it was relatively measured. My aggression only dealt in scratches or in bruises, but never in dislocated joints, for example, and much less in broken bones. No, nothing about my past conduct could explain the portrait I had seen that would now haunt me forever. For my past mistakes I deserved a half dozen moles at most, and small ones. Or eyes less crossed. Or ears only slightly large. No more than that. All the rest was due to some other cause, an external cause. I was a victim, not the villain. But a victim of what?

After mulling it over, I found the guilty party: my mother. That quiet, skittish woman was afraid of everything, of the wind, of thunderstorms, but more than anything she feared my father, who treated her like crap. She never let herself get close to me. Sometimes she would tell me a story; sometimes she would sing me a lullaby in her awful voice; sometimes she would caress my cheek, but with a wary, trembling hand. And that about summed up our relationship. Having seen the mirror, I could now identify the reason for her behavior. She avoided me because of my ugliness, but also, I concluded, after much contemplation on the matter, because of the guilt she must have felt, the guilt to which my ugliness bore witness.

But guilty of what? Searching for the answer to this question, I remembered something she had told me when I was still a kid. When she was pregnant with me, she used to contemplate the rocky, scarred mountain that dominated the landscape in our desolate region. She had made the comment in a forcedly casual tone meant to cloak her underlying apprehension, which probably neither she nor I perceived at the time. But now, in retrospect, her apprehension spoke volumes. Because there on the mountain was the explanation for my ugliness, there, on that hostile geographic mishap I knew all too well. It was a place where an elusive girl like myself would go to seek refuge, perhaps moved, it now occurred to me, by a certain discretionary affinity that the ghastly traits of my physiognomy shared on a smaller but no less atrocious scale with the tortured landscape. A protruding boulder was my nose; the dark entrance to one of the many caves corresponded to my mouth. Many people see faces in clouds. I saw in the mountain—that monument to the freakish—the reproduction of my own face. The impressions my mother had had during gestation were permanently chiseled onto the face of her daughter. A daughter she surely did not want; at that time my dad was after another woman. He had impregnated his wife so that she couldn't interfere in his shameful romance. Tears streaking down her face, my scorned and pregnant mother spent her days staring at the mountain. She knew that up there, concealed in some cave, her lewd husband was screwing all the livelong day; she hoped to catch him emerging from his hiding place, exhausted and satisfied, to at least give him the stink eye. She even pulled it off a time or two, but it had no effect: The man didn't give a shit about her stink eye. Her obsessive vigilance did, however, have an unexpected effect: The image of the mountain was forever imprinted on my face. Like those moms who eat strawberries and their kid is born with a birthmark in the exact shape of a strawberry.

An unexpected consequence. Hmm . . . I don't know if it was all that unexpected. Hadn't my mom been guided by a hidden purpose in her obsessive conduct? The little cretin is cheating on me, so I'll get my revenge on him by inscribing on his son's face the same cruel impressions that he left on my heart (my dad wanted a boy for his firstborn; in fact, he only wanted boys, but Jehovah punished him with three daughters, the first one butt ugly). And with that rationale she fixated on the rocks in hopes of an unsightly child. My face, the metaphoric allusion to the mountain where my father had sinned, would constitute a perpetual memento, an insistent accusation in continual protest against his infidelity that was, in the end, a charge against lust. It worked: I came out ugly as sin.

How traumatized my father must have been when he took me in his arms. The horror! The horror!

The real question is, Why didn't he kill me? Stories circulated among our people, told in hushed voices, of parents who offed their children by throwing them from the top of the mountain into a pit with as many bones as rocks. A firstborn daughter was always an inconvenience, to say the least. She didn't guarantee succession, didn't help out at work, and would need a dowry to get married. Now, a firstborn ugly daughter was even worse than that. She was a tragedy whose fate could only be the precipice.

My father didn't kill me. His motive, I can't be sure of. Perhaps he suffered as well, out of guilt—guilt was the main component of our tradition. In all the stories our elders told, there was always a merciless god accusing us of something. Apart from that, it's possible my father felt some sort of remorse because, unlike my mom, the other woman had zero respect for him. She'd let the cat out of the bag that he was an incompetent lover. So he accepted the mute accusation portrayed on the face of his newborn daughter.

I grew uglier and uglier. And remained ignorant of my ugliness. Due to a lack of mirrors, obviously, but I could have supplemented that lack. In nature there is no want of reflective surfaces. A puddle of water, for example, makes a good mirror, although with inconvenient distortions (merciful distortions, in my case) caused by ripples. And the eyes of others, could they not have indirectly served as mirrors? The expressions of surprise, or even of horror, that I saw, or believed I had seen, in the faces of people who looked at me, shouldn't they have been enough of a hint? Even if I were blind (God, how I wished I were blind after having seen myself in the mirror), nothing should have kept me from seeing the truth. Touching my face should have been enough; with fingers even half knowing what to look for, exploring its grotesque contours and startling asymmetries should have been enough. But I never did. I have pretty hands. (Indeed, I have nice breasts, good hips—I am of that paradoxical variety of woman known as butterface: Everything looks good but her face.) Yet, my hands, as if moving of their own accord, refused to tour the dreary country that was my face. I would try to convince them: Come on, hands, explore my mouth and nose, fear not my uncharted waters, fortune favors the bold, no risk no reward. But my hands were smarter than their owner. No, they would say, we'll mind our own business. Your face is not our beach, we refuse to vacation there. There's not a tourist package out there you could sell us. We prefer to stay put, engaged in daily chores like cooking, washing, cleaning—or, in the best of circumstances, caressing your breasts—those soft rolling hills we're so fond of. That's how my hands went on pretending, letting it be, taking it easy, insisting it's all good—their silent conspiracy, in the end. Clever hands. In our part of the world, cutting off the hands of thieves and sexual deviants was a common punishment. My hands had not committed a serious enough crime, but their acts of omission were certainly objectionable.

That it had taken eighteen years of my life to finally diagnose my ugliness is a testament to how much human beings, with or without the help of others, are capable of self-delusion. And it also goes to show how strong of a temptation a little white lie can be. My sister, for example, did not give up on repairing the disastrous damage caused by the mirror incident. She came to talk to me the next morning. She told me a story as well intentioned as it was ill conceived, a story that surely cost her a full night's sleep. She asserted that, after careful examination, she had detected cracks in the mirror, cracks that she hadn't noticed before and that had certainly altered my reflection. I oughtn't, therefore, worry. Everything I had seen was nothing but an erroneous impression that a slightly less imperfect mirror would take care of fixing.

I had to hand it to her for doing everything under the sun to convince me. But she was unsuccessful. What she possessed in sympathy (and in guilt) she lacked in the ability to lie. She stammered, avoided eye contact. To spare her, I also lied.

"That must be it," I exclaimed, in a tone more convincing than hers. "Never trust a mirror of suspicious quality. I knew it. I knew I couldn't be that dreadful."

For her part she was relieved, grateful. Not me. Lies aside, my fate was sealed. I was now the ugly girl, and everything in my life would be conditioned by my ugliness. No man would want me. No man would sing of my beauty in sentimental lyrics. My love life would be as dry as the desert that surrounded us.

I won't deny it: I thought about killing myself. All I had to do was climb the mountain and throw myself off. My body would smash against the rocks below, the vultures would devour my flesh and entrails, the sun would bleach my bones where they had been destined to lie since the dawn of time.

I didn't kill myself. In the first place, I didn't have the guts. After the fact, suicide, besides being looked down upon (isn't it amazing how even we ugly girls internalize the attitudes of the dominant culture?) wouldn't solve my problem. I would cease to be ugly in life, but who could guarantee that my ugliness hadn't also compromised my skull? Nothing would stop some future member of an archaeological expedition from digging up my cranium and, after gazing upon it with horror, exclaiming to a colleague: "What a terrible thing it must have been to be this woman; that's not a face, it's an offense!" Scientific impartiality doesn't preclude aesthetic sensibilities.

No. I would stick it out until the end with my face. Ideally alone, where I wouldn't have to endure looks of horror, of fear, of sadness, of sympathy—but yes, I would stick it out until the end.

I became a hermit. A part-time hermit, but a hermit nonetheless. Since I had no other option, I slept in my family's house, but no sooner did the sun come up than I would book it to the mountain, up until then a sanctuary for the goats that escaped my father's herd (and, like I said, his own sex haven from time to time). However, unlike full-time hermits, who just want to get away from the rest of humanity, I was in search of something. And when I found it, I immediately knew it was what I'd been looking for.

A stone. A small stone.

Unlike other rocks on the mountain, this one was gentle and smooth to the touch. So smooth it surprised me. What sort of erosion had wiped away its roughness?

Who knows, maybe it wasn't erosion. Maybe it was the work of some mysterious mountain dweller, like a gnome or wizard, who had patiently polished its once-rough surface, thinking, One day the ugly one will come to the mountain in desperation and then this stone will give her solace.

I don't know. One thing is for sure: The stone—with its size, its egg shape, and more than anything its smoothness—would get the job done. The stone would be a substitute for the lover that ugly me would never have. Introduced into my vagina, it would make me come.

I had no other choice. From that day on, my good stone provided me with many moments of bitter, solitary pleasure. Hidden among other normal-looking, coarse rocks, my beloved little stone would wait for me, impatient, anticipating the spelunking that was to come in my humid little grotto, trembling, yes, with pleasure. What's that? You don't think stones feel? O ye deceived ones! O ye men and women of little faith! Of course stones can feel. They feel more than certain humans with hardened hearts. They just don't show their feelings. They don't shout, cry, or clamor to the heavens. But they react with gratitude to the hand that caresses them, storing up tenderness like a battery stores energy, and then they return the favor. In my case, in the case of my beloved stone, we're talking high returns that pay interest and dividends. My, oh my, what orgasms, ladies and gentlemen! What orgasms! Truly earthshattering, culminating in a piercing and unrestrained moan.

I could've been happy with turning my back on the world and all its wiles. But no, I wasn't immune to temptation. I ended up in the gutter with everyone else. The gutter of human sentiment, that is.

I fell in love.

There was a shepherd boy who worked for my father and happened to tend his flocks on the mountain trails. I caught sight of him every day. He was a handsome young man, tall and strong. He would sing nostalgic melodies of star-crossed love in his beautiful voice. I'd never paid him much mind. In our village he had a reputation for being a weirdo. The other shepherds mocked him, saying he was a goatfucker, which could even be true. One way or another lonely people find an outlet for their passions, a goat or a stone will do whenever make-believe is needed to surmount a sad reality. Make-believe or otherwise, the dude definitely seemed a bit off to me. Up to that point, we had maybe exchanged half a dozen words, if we'd spoken at all.

Now, however, I saw the shepherd boy in a new light. And it was exactly in that light that I began to have certain ideas... certain hope... The two of us alone together, on the mountain. Would he fall into temptation? Yes, I was ugly, but no uglier than the goats he herded, even though there were a few nice females in their ranks, of a breed I can no longer recall. But I was sure I could beat out the competition. At the very least I would fit nicely into his arms. At the very least I could whisper sweet nothings in his ear, something no goat could do.

One day I mustered the courage to confront him: "Come here, let's talk." At first he deflected, said he couldn't, but eventually he gave in to my advances: "Take a seat, let's have a lively chat." To my surprise, he was a pleasant guy. And curious: He wanted to know what the boss's daughter was doing holed up on the mountain. I immediately made up a story, and a good one at that. I told him an angel had appeared to me in a dream and brought me a message from the Lord: I would find the man of my dreams on the mountain trails, grazing goats. He heard me out, intrigued, but he didn't get my insinuation, the simpleton. Pressing on, I showed him the cave and said that it would be the ideal place to live out a great love affair.

His reaction was surprising. "The cave," he exclaimed, slapping his forehead, "why didn't I think of the cave before? I'm such an idiot, but she'll like this idea."

"She who?" I asked.

Well, who else but my sister, obviously. The pretty one. The flirt. Without me knowing, without anyone knowing, they had been dating for some time. He'd won her over with the object of her desire and my disgrace: the mirror, which he had stolen. Whenever opportunity knocks, shepherds rarely blink twice when it comes to abandoning their flocks to raid caravans passing through the area.

Their love had yet to be consummated for one reason: They didn't have a place where they could safely hook up. The cave would easily solve their problem. That's why he was so grateful to me when I mentioned it. He told me the whole story, asked me to help him out.

I agreed. What else could I do? I agreed. I forsook love instantaneously, but I agreed.

That very afternoon, my sister sprinted up the mountain trail. Like her boyfriend, she thanked me for the leg up I was giving them. The Lord shall repay you, she promised me. Here on the mountain you, too, shall find your beloved. (Who? Who, little sister, who? My polished stone? An old billy goat? The angel of the Lord? Ouch, little sister, you could have spared me the patronizing prophecy.)

They asked me to keep an eye on the trails so that they would not be disturbed—a mission I accomplished very well. I stood guard at the entrance of the cave. Deep inside, where it's cold, the shepherd boy had lit a fire. All I could see were their silhouettes jumping with the flames, contorting themselves in a bout of sex gymnastics. And moaning and shouting and laughing.... My tears went unnoticed.

It didn't end well. My father wised up to what was going on. He was furious when he found out his daughter had been deflowered by an employee. As patriarch, he gathered together the entire village and gave summary public judgment (minus a defense attorney; no one dared take on that role). The miserable little shepherd boy was found guilty and condemned. He would receive the punishment favored by desert tribes: a good old-fashioned stoning. A large quantity of mountain stones was immediately provided. Tied to a stake, the boy made an easy target for the stones cast furiously by the village men. I watched helplessly as I consoled my poor sister who, terrified, didn't know what to do. The stones finally ran out. An inch from death, bleeding profusely, the boy was untied and sent packing.

"Get lost," my father said, "I don't ever want to see you around here again. Show your face again and next time you'll be stoned to death."

He staggered off, limping.

My sister quickly got over him, mostly because she already had her eye on another shepherd boy. Ever the opportunist, my father promised the guy twenty goats, on the condition that he assume paternity of the baby that was on the way. The townspeople also felt no regret over the whole stoning episode; according to them, the transgressor had had it coming. To the point that soon no one talked about him, not even his parents.

The only one who suffered—and suffered in silence—was me. The shepherd boy was my only hope, as absurd a hope as it was, of loving and being loved. I was alone, with my stone.

But was masturbation all I was up to?

No. That wasn't the only thing. Okay, yes, it was all I was doing, until the scribe took pity on me.

The scribe was the only man my father respected. For one simple reason: He was the only one among us who knew how to read and write. He was not, therefore, just another employee. He earned more, had special rights; for example, he received a monthly supply of goat cheese, a rare and highly valued delicacy. But his assignments were also special. My father entrusted him with the dispatches from the king. Such dispatches, although uncommon, were always urgent because they contained tax obligations. It was up to the scribe to answer them, a task that demanded not only control over the written word but considerable political savvy—my father's relationship with the Crown was not the best. The scribe was also responsible for keeping a sort of accounting of my father's herds and other assets, not to mention the tributes that the patriarch collected. In the village, the scribe was respected and feared. They considered him a sort of magician.

Now, he was ugly, the old man. God, was he ugly! The age difference aside, in ugliness we were rivals. Maybe that's where his soft spot for me came from. He was always gifting me things: a loaf of bread, a piece of goat cheese. And, whenever he could, he told me stories. He knew everything about our tribe's past.

One day he called me to the tent that served as his office.

"Come here," he said, with an air of mystery. "I want to talk to you."

I confess that initially I had dirty thoughts. Had the moment finally come when my stone would be substituted for a cock, a real albeit an elderly one? Somewhat scared but also somewhat excited, I went into his tent. Inside there was nothing but a small table and a rustic bench. We stood there, him looking at me in a strange way. It's happening, I thought, he's going to tell me to strip down.

But no.

"I am going," he announced in a solemn but shaky voice, "to teach you to write."

Now that was truly a surprising turn of events, the most surprising turn that had ever turned in my life. Writing was something for the chosen few, for people who, through obscure mechanisms, learned to master a skill that the rest of us looked up to with almost religious reverence. Not only that—a woman scribe? Impossible. A woman, even an ugly one, was meant to take care of the house, get married, make babies. What he was proposing, though shy of transgression, was something quite out of the ordinary. It could cost him dearly. What would my father say when he found out about this proposal? It was something I didn't want to think about. He held the scribe in high regard, depended on him, but if ever his authority were questioned, he would not hesitate to make an example of the old man, along the lines of a stoning, or worse.

And yet the scribe was serious. Yes, he wanted to teach me to write. Why? I don't know. Out of pity, perhaps: The poor girl is ugly, she'll never find a man, she needs reimbursement, a means of escape from her frustration. Or out of some premonition—the future, as you will see, had a surprise in store for me that perhaps he foresaw. Whatever the case, the truth is he had me sit at the table and showed me how to use writing utensils like quill, ink, parchment. Before I knew it, I was tracing the first letter of the alphabet—the aleph, which marks the beginning of everything.

What a rush. God, what a thrill! I surveyed my chicken scratch with the satisfaction of an artist contemplating her masterpiece. I had attained something I never dreamed of. What's more, it changed me in a short space of time. I didn't feel so ugly anymore. My face was the same, but the sensation of intrinsic ugliness, the sensation that had followed me into my dreams and transformed them into nightmares from which I would awake screaming, that sensation had faded considerably. I was now . . . ugly-*ish*. A perfectly tolerable condition that, compared to what I had experienced, represented a new stage of unexpected well-being, of happiness almost. I felt light, free, as if the act of writing—one letter, one single letter—had liberated me from an oppressive past. I began to talk compulsively about my childhood, about my fantasies, about my aspirations. I talked and talked, and the scribe listened, smiling.

And then it happened: Overwhelmed with elation—the whole writing thing, for some obscure reason, rekindled my passions—I threw myself into his arms and made my offer: "Take me, I'm yours!" He rejected me delicately: No, he couldn't have relations with me. It wasn't right to take advantage of my gratitude, and, even if he wanted to, he couldn't; for some time he had been unacquainted with sex. His helping me implied no ulterior motives. He had acted exclusively out of solidarity, sympathy, and a desire to teach. He was old and wanted to pass on his knowledge of writing, and it seemed to him that I was the right person.

It was all very noble, but I suspected that, deep down, he wasn't so detached. More than once I had noticed the rancor on his face when my father gave him some order or another. Was he not attempting to subvert the familial order of patriarchy, weaponizing the ugly firstborn daughter through an activity reserved for men, and for only a select number of men?

Little did it matter to me. Having discovered the world of the written word, I was happy, very happy. Hidden away in my mountain cave, I spent days writing by tenuous lamplight (my ability would have to remain a secret, at the scribe's behest). Writing what? Anything. Thoughts. Verses. Stories, above all stories. Stories I made up in which I was always the beautiful heroine whose attention some prince, charming or otherwise, jockeyed for. True stories, stories about our people, which the scribe would tell me and I would transcribe on parchment. He would speak of my father, a handsome and vigorous man, a leader who led his people through the desert to an oasis near a mountain: Here we shall build our houses, here we shall found a great city. Writing about my father, I somehow rose above him; I was a wise and powerful woman, he a bewildered and scared child. But the narrative stopped where it began. To continue it I would need his approval, which he would never give me. My story is in my head, I imagined him saying, enraged, I'll tell it when I'm good and ready.

It made no difference to me. The act of writing was enough. Placing letter after letter on the parchment, word after word, was something that delighted me. It wasn't just a text that I was producing, it was beauty, beauty born of order and harmony. I discovered that one letter attracts another, that one word attracts another, their kinship organizing not just a text but also life, the universe. What I beheld on the parchment when I concluded my work was a map, like those celestial maps that indicate the position of stars and planets, their positioning determined not by some chance outcome but by the composition of mysterious forces, the same ones that, to a lesser degree, guided my hand as it left ciphers on parchment. It was about power, a power that I was slowly taking on. An intoxicating experience that I could not share with anyone; my mother would die from shock if she found out, my sisters would eat their hearts out with envy. The only person I had any desire to tell about my experience was the shepherd boy. I would tell him that my life made sense now, that it had meaning. Ugly I might be, but I was capable of creating beauty. Not the false beauty reflected in deceptive mirrors, but the true and everlasting beauty of the words I wrote, day after day, week after week, as if I were in a state of permanent and delicious inebriation.

Yes, I felt transported to another world, another reality. Everything was forgotten. Even the stone? Yes, unbelievers, even the stone. The stone? What use was the stone? What use was fantasy if the fantasy was now within my reach, me being able to conjure it at any moment?

Thinking about the stone was something I rarely did. Mostly it filled me with remorse—a remorse so intense that one time I couldn't resist going to my hiding place to see if it was still there where I had left it. At first, when I didn't find it, I started to panic. I immediately thought that someone had taken it. But who? And why? Had the stone—with its oval shape, its smooth surface—ended up a decorative curiosity in someone's house, or had whoever found it put it to other uses? A thousand things occurred to me: the stone landing in the hands of my father and him calling me, furious: "Do you recognize this stone, and if so, what were you doing with it?"

No, no one had pilfered my stone. I'd looked in the wrong spot. When I found it I began crying for joy. I kissed it, asked for its forgiveness. And suddenly, I felt the urge.... A painful dilemma: on the one hand, my stone and the meager yet reassuring comfort that it offered me; on the other, my new status as a lettered sophisticate, obviously incompatible with such base instincts. However, the temptation was too strong, and I knew I would give in—but at that exact moment a great fuss rose from the village below. It's the shepherd boy returned, I immediately thought. He came back to challenge my father and the village and take me with him, me, the only woman he ever loved. Driven by my harebrained idea, I threw the stone into the cave and rushed down the mountain.

No, it wasn't the return of my shepherd boy. It was an emissary of the king who had come to town, as he periodically did. This was always a big occasion. He would enter the village to the sound of trumpets and drums, escorted by a healthy contingent of armed soldiers. We would receive him with frenetic applause, which poorly masked our general terror: The emissary was almost always a bearer of bad news. He either came to collect back taxes, impose new laws, or recruit young men for war. Despite it all, my father aways demanded that the tribe treat the man well, with tributes and offerings. He didn't want trouble with the king. Such a thing could cost him dearly.

When I got to the village, gasping for breath, the emissary—a fat and sweaty man—was struggling to get off his camel. He complimented everyone present and, after a suspenseful moment, solemnly announced that he brought a message from the king. Like everyone else there, I thought it would be another one of his usual communiqués, especially since it was tax season. Alas, I was wrong. The scroll that the emissary produced from his finely embroidered silk bag would forever change my life.

My father received the message and, as was the custom, handed it to his scribe, who unrolled it and read carefully.

He immediately grew pale, which only made our apprehension grow. Evidently it was something really important and, by the looks of things, outside the habitual norm, because in a low voice he said that he needed to consult my father alone.

The emissary was not happy. Impatient, he warned that according to the king's orders he had to return immediately.

"And with my mission accomplished," he added in the tone of a thinly veiled threat.

My father followed the scribe into his tent and for some time they remained there. I could hear muffled interjections, but I hadn't the faintest idea what they were talking about. My father finally emerged. He came my way, looking at me in a strange way that expressed contradictory feelings: joy, but also vexation and perhaps even revulsion. He tried to say something but was unable get the words out. With an angry gesture, he turned to his scribe and asked him to give me the news. Then he walked off, taking everyone there with him. Now I was no longer intrigued—I was terrified. So, the message was about me? But of what interest could I, the ugly one, the insignificant one, be to the powerful monarch who governed us?

"Come with me," said the scribe, pushing aside the tent flap.

"What's all this about?" I asked in a shaky voice. In response, he handed me the scroll adorned with the garish seal of the king.

"Read it yourself. Now that you know how."

I read. At first, I couldn't believe what I held before my eyes.

"In accordance to our tradition and the law," the letter said, "thou art hereby summoned to concede thine eldest daughter as a wife to the king, in order that the alliance between the royal house and thy tribe may be strengthened." The eldest daughter: me. I had been chosen to be a wife to the king. Me, who had never known a man, me, who minutes prior had been wavering between masturbation and sublimation, was set to marry the most powerful man in the kingdom. Maybe even the world. I didn't know what to say. I didn't know whether to laugh or to cry. I didn't know whether to jump for joy or to throw myself to the floor and throw a tantrum. I stood there stock-still, paralyzed.

My fathered returned to the tent and glared at me in silence. Now I understood the confusion of feelings that had overcome him and been translated into the look on his face. On the one hand, he felt rewarded, flattered. The marriage, as the letter said, was a political alliance—and an alliance with the king was the one thing every tribal leader coveted, my father more than anyone, mostly because he faced multiple threats, both foreign and domestic. He had long feared an attack from neighboring tribes, envious of our lovely goats and sheep. On the other hand, his leadership of the tribe was not the strongest. There was stiff opposition from many family heads, not to mention open disrespect from some of the young people. The episode with the shepherd had been the final straw. True, we were talking about a slightly troubled boy, but in times past no one would have dared deflower the patriarch's own daughter, much less in the same cave that the patriarch used for his own affairs, which also elicited mockery. He nevertheless stood to enjoy special protection once he allied with the throne; his status would improve, not to mention that his debts would surely be forgiven, or at least refinanced at a lower rate, in the ballpark of two or three percent annually, depending, quite naturally, on his credit score. His daughter would have a life of luxury and comfort at the royal palace. True, she would be but one among hundreds of wives and concubines, and she would be a prisoner in a gilded cage for the remainder of her life, far from the village, far from him. What he couldn't shake off was that, in the end, he had raised me. I was his daughter. Despite our differences, deep down there was some affection between us and, who knows, ugliness aside, maybe even complicity. All things considered, however, the king's order looked to be very favorable for him and, possibly, for me.

Now: there was just one problem... a potentially serious problem.... What if the king rejected me? What if he sent me back saying, "I don't do ugly. That woman is no wife, she's an affront. You thought you could throw out the garbage for an alliance pledge?" That would really create a thorny problem. Whether by the king or not, my father couldn't accept my being returned, which inevitably would be characterized as an offense, or worse, a mockery—after all, as his daughter, I was the fruit of his loins, product of the patriarch. Showing any sign of protest would be, under the circumstances, a complicated thing. What could he do? Resort to civil disobedience, refuse to pay taxes? Go for outright revolt and join one of the rebel groups that—presently few and far between—fought against centralized power?

A sticky situation. But my father—who wasn't our leader for nothing, who had some political acumen—didn't want to be overhasty. At the moment his priority was to set things straight with me, his daughter. Of course, as my father, he could command me to submit to his will and marry the king. But he hoped I would agree to it, or at least not make a scene, which would be very unpleasant and demand of him forceful if not violent intervention—something incompatible with the cheerful mood that supposedly ought to characterize an engagement. He looked at me expectantly: The ball was in my court.

At that moment I was overcome with terror. I felt like a child afraid of the dark all over again. If I could, I would have grabbed hold of him and, in tears, implored him, "Don't let them take me, please. I want to stay with you, with Mommy and my little sisters." But I couldn't do that. I wanted to spare him, it's true—after all, he was my father—but it wasn't just that, it was my pride. I had long since learned to hide my emotions. It was bad enough I was ugly. Crying would transform me into something far scarier. So I held it in and said, dryly and with dignity, that I would accept his will.

It was more than he could have asked for, much more. He hugged me with excitement. It wasn't the type of hug reserved for his women in the cave, but it was a hug nevertheless, and we emerged from the tent in an embrace to tell everyone the good news. Naturally, it caused a sensation: My choice was a big deal for the village. Everyone came out to hug me. "I knew that everything would turn out okay," whispered my sister. She pretended to be happy for me, barely containing her jealousy: She got a shepherd boy for twenty goats, and for free, I got a king. Now I would have all the mirrors I ever wanted. Plus, I could even become beautiful—there would be no lack of resources at the palace for such an undertaking.

Our departure was scheduled for the next morning. That afternoon I gathered what few things I possessed and, for the last time, ascended the mountain to watch the sun set over the desert. I went to my hiding place, grabbed my stone, and said goodbye. I would no longer need my dildo, which had faithfully accompanied me in so many of my fantasies. "Goodbye, my beloved stone," I muttered, truly moved. As a final tribute, I deposited it in the back of the cave that had set the stage of passion for my father and the shepherd boy, and for my own passion—writing.

That night I could hardly sleep, such was my restlessness. Overcome with exhaustion, I finally managed to fall asleep when early morning came, and then I had a strange dream. I was in an unknown place, a great hall, which could only be the hall of a royal palace. Size was a luxury. On the wall at the other end was an immense mirror. I ran to look at myself and what I saw was not my reflection, but that of another woman very different than me: tall, pretty, with olive skin and an enigmatic smile. I wanted to ask her who she was, what she was doing there, but I ran out of time when my father abruptly woke me up. The king's emissary was ready to leave. I got dressed in a hurry, quickly bade farewell to my family, and that was that. The next thing I knew we were on the road, headed for the capital. A long and difficult journey not without danger: The misery of recent times had provoked an increase in attacks from gangs opposed to the king.

I traveled confined in a small tent mounted on the back of a camel, for as the king's property, not a soul could lay eyes on me. Theoretically, I too was forbidden from looking at anything, but by the second day I grew tired of my splendid isolation and parted the tent flaps just enough to peer through without getting caught. At first, all I saw was desert, an arid landscape that was familiar to me. The desert had engendered me, raised me. The desert was my home turf. The home I was leaving behind.

Soon the scenery began to change. Larger and larger villages sprang up, populated with people from other tribes, people I didn't know, wearing strange clothing—all cause for surprise and distress. God, the world was so big. And I was so far from my house! Then, on the fourth day of our journey, I spotted a familiar figure on the road that made my heart skip a beat: my shepherd boy. He was walking with difficulty, a limp, and, worst of all, his face was disfigured from the stoning he took. My poor shepherd boy, what had my father's punishment reduced him to? I wanted to call out to him, invite him into my small tent. In its rather cozy enclosure we would find room for the intimacy that for so long I had desired. We would talk, exchange looks, and who knows, maybe even . . .

Out of the question. I now belonged to the king. I had to forget my beloved little shepherd boy. Plus, maybe he didn't need my help. True, he had been humiliated and beaten to a pulp and shamefully banished, but on the bright side he was now free to wander wherever the wind might take him. He could woo as many maidens (or goats) as he wanted, and all the while I would be confined to the royal palace. Our paths were diverging, so much so that my camel, being the faster of the two, soon left the hobbling shepherd boy behind, eating our dust.

As we got closer to our destination, doubt began to creep into my mind. What would the palace be like? What would the harem be like? And—above all—what would the man be like to whom my body, my life, would soon belong? I hadn't the faintest idea, but my anxiety had me on pins and needles. I was about to live an adventure, an adventure full of twists and turns. That feeling grew sharper as the road ascended and we drew closer to the legendary capital. Behind me lay the desert, my solitary mountain; behind me lay my past. Ahead was my future, my golden age. One morning I awoke and there it was before my very eyes, Jerusalem, with its towers and city walls.

Jerusalem. Ever since I was a kid the name had sparked my imagination. Mostly because I had never been there. My father spoke of a great and beautiful city, a place where one lived with intensity. My sisters and I would listen to him in astonished and resigned silence. We had little chance of ever making the almost mythical journey there; the royal city, the city of the Temple, it was a place for men's pilgrimages, not for women's. Happy were the daughters of Jerusalem, those born there; the rest had to make do with stories from travelers. But now I was there, not just as a visitor, but as a chosen wife of the king. Daughters of Jerusalem, I wanted to shout, bow down before me!

The caravan's arrival caused quite the stir. In the narrow streets we traversed, an actual multitude gathered to watch us pass by. I won't lie, a bit of pride swelled within me when I realized my tent was the cause of so much interest and excitement. Everyone knew that inside that tent was the king's new wife, whom they surely imagined to be a beautiful seductress. They were wrong, but they would never know it because they would never see me. I would never set foot outside the royal palace.

We now reached said palace, imposing and luxurious. We passed through the gates, guarded by sentinels, entered the courtyard, and there the caravan stopped. The king's emissary, with whom I hadn't exchanged a word the entire journey, came to help me down and present me to the harem overseer, who would take care of me from then on. The woman was big and fat and strong, with a masculine way about her (maybe she participated in the pleasures of the seraglio). She looked at me, intrigued. I knew what she was thinking: God, this is an ugly one, the ugliest in the bunch. But if she thought it, she of course didn't say it. From then on, no one would call me ugly. I was now the king's wife. She limited herself to greeting me with conventional small talk. Next she wanted to know if I was tired. I said no, that the journey had been nice.

"Well then," she said, "we can save some time by filling out paperwork."

She explained: Since the harem was so big, a basic system of registry was necessary, largely because the king knew little about his future wives. She gave me a veil—my face would never again be seen by any man except for the king, or those he authorized. Then she took me to the office of Solomon's head scribe, a hunched-over old man who, with a grumpy look and nasally voice, asked me something that I didn't understand (I was beginning to suspect reading and writing was not a young man's game). I asked him to repeat the question.

"I asked if you were the newcomer!" he shouted. Regaining his composure, he welcomed me and inquired whether he could create my file, a routine thing—again, I had to sit through the story about the basic administrative organization necessary for such a large harem with so many wives and concubines. I said sure, that I was at his service to provide whatever information he wanted. Quite satisfied, he unrolled a scroll on the table—my file—grabbed his quill, dipped it in the inkwell, and began.

"Full name."

I said my name. He continued his inquiry: date of birth, filiation, names of siblings and other relatives, mailing address, the usual stuff; and other things not so usual, like dietary preferences and favorite colors. He also wanted to know if I sang, danced, or recited poetry. He asked me to narrate, off the cuff, my most recent dream, or in case I didn't remember, any daydream I'd had. I went about answering while he, sitting at his desk in front of me, wrote laboriously. I noticed he misspelled the word *dream* and, after briefly hesitating, I showed him his error.

He looked at me as if I were from another planet.

"But you know how to read and write, then?" he asked in amazement.

I said yes and told him how I had learned. He made a long footnote about it and then looked at me with reverence but also with a bit of anger, which didn't go unnoticed. Well, let him be angry with me, I thought. Soon my marriage to the king will be consummated and then I'll take a shit on this old fart's head.

Having completed the necessary paperwork, I was taken to the priest's office. The high-ranking member of the Temple hierarchy ushered me in and ordered the harem overseer to leave us.

"I am not to be disturbed," he added in a severe tone.

Turning to me, he asked if I knew why I had been brought into his presence. I answered that I awaited instructions regarding the ceremony that, in my head, still ought to take place that day, despite not seeing preparations of any kind. He looked at me with an air of superiority and said it was nothing of the sort. His task was actually something else. He had to certify that I was not a bearer of injury, that I showed no sign of impurity—ultimately, of leprosy, that disease which was a curse upon those who contracted it. I had to strip naked, obviously, but fear not, for I stood before a holy man who had long ago freed himself from lust. Without hesitation—orders from on high are not to be deliberated—I took off my clothes. He looked me up and down. He said nothing, for obvious reasons, but I knew what he was thinking: Nice body that one, the king will have a good time.

He examined me meticulously and found nothing. But then he remembered to have me take off the veil, according to the harem overseer's instructions. And there he trembled, visibly shaking. He couldn't take his eyes off my face.

Etched on his face, I saw repulsion and fasciation. Repulsed by my ugliness, fascinated by my moles, a kaleidoscope of skin tags the likes of which he, a man with encyclopedic knowledge of skin abnormalities, had never seen. He went to work studying my moles one by one, jotting down notes and sketches on parchment. I had ceased to interest him. What mattered was my small wart whose shape vaguely reminded him of an insect he'd once seen on a tree by the Sea of Galilee.... He muttered under his breath and took notes, took notes and under his breath muttered. Finally, sick of the same old story, I excused myself, dressed, and left—to the obvious disappointment of the priest, who hadn't yet finished his note-taking.

I was directed to the harem, adjacent to the palace and separated from it by a small courtyard with palm trees and bubbling fountains. Like the palace, the harem was beyond anything I could have imagined in the way of material luxury. A vast pavilion, richly decorated with silk curtains, soft rugs, and exotic plants in vases. Even peacocks, the vainest of birds, formed part of the scenery.

And, naturally, there were the women. It came as a shock to see them. Of course, I knew beforehand that Solomon had the largest harem in the world, but one thing is knowing, it's another entirely to see it with your own eyes. God, what an enormous flock of women gathered in one place! An abundance of women, bushels of women, women in bulk, women to spare and to sell, an absurdity of women, a womanly flood. Women standing, sitting, or lying around; conversing, laughing, smiling; meditative women and even (but only in one case) in tears. Women eating, women playing the flute, women smelling flowers. Women by themselves, women in pairs, in groups of three or more. Women in squadrons, women in battle formations, a lineup of women, women in circles, in triangles (isosceles and scalene), in rectangles. Talkative women, serious women, worked-up women, laid-back women. As for their beauty (and how could I not notice this little item), they came in drop-dead gorgeous, very pretty, reasonably pretty, agreeable. But ugly, not a one of them. Not even one. Perhaps I could label a nose or two as imperfect, a mouth or two as poorly shaped, but ugliness like mine, complete, definitive, there was not. I was, alas, the only one.

It was easy to distinguish the wives as such from the concubines, who dressed in a simpler manner and presented themselves modestly (maybe a bit tongue-in-cheek, but at any rate modesty predominated). The concubines, possibly out of constraint, ignored my presence. But the wives watched me attentively. Without a doubt they feared the new arrival could become the king's favorite. But now, without my veil, a quick glance my way was enough to convince them that I was not the enemy. In our race for the royal heart, in pole position I was not—to the contrary, I was caught at a standstill, falling farther behind. Relieved, they began to laugh. They took one look at me, one look at my face, and they were like, What hole did she crawl out of? Snickering, at first only snickering, then cackling, guffawing—spitting jeers, total disrespect. Solidarity, ça va sans dire, not a chance. Just look at that dumpster fire. She wasn't birthed, she was shat out. If I had a heart condition I would have died just now—and so on.

I didn't say a word. I could have reacted. I could have busted the faces of half a dozen of those namby-pambies, because what I lacked in beauty I made up for in muscles, and many a girl in my village had felt the wrath of my fists. But I wasn't in the mood to cause a kerfuffle. Not at that moment, at least. So I sucked it up and let myself be led by the harem overseer, who tried to console me as best she could: "Don't listen to them, they're just jealous, they like to tease their colleagues." She took me to a room where several slaves assumed my care, bathing me, perfuming me, and finally dressing me up like a true odalisque. When they finished, the woman told me to have a look at myself in the large hanging mirror. I hesitated—another disappointment in front of its polished surface would be more than I could bear. She, however, insisted: "Come, look at your transformation."

I stood in front of the mirror, eyes closed. I took a deep breath, counted to three, and opened them.

Okay, that was a surprise. A very pleasant surprise. The girls had actually done a pretty good job. The silk garb, semitransparent, brought attention to my body, which, as I said, wasn't half bad. Then there was the veil, a thick veil that hid my face, lending me an air at once prudent and seductive. A screened-in porch, great idea.

They asked me what I thought. The way they treated me, I should add, was extremely respectful—after all, I was a wife to the king. I said I was pleased, that my expectations had in fact been surpassed.

"Very well," said the harem overseer. "If it is to your liking, then follow me to the throne room."

The moment had arrived, my big moment. As I followed the woman down the long corridors, closer and closer to the throne room, everything else, my whole life up to that moment, faded into the past. My father, my mother, my family, my little shepherd boy, my stone (poor stone), everything now was but a memory. I was entering a new phase in my life.

We finally arrived. The massive doors, guarded by armed soldiers, were closed.

"We'll have to wait a bit," said the woman.

After some time, which to me was unbearably long, the doors opened and a white-bearded man dressed in fancy clothing appeared. One of the courtiers.

"She's the one?" he asked dryly.

"She's the one," responded the harem overseer. "Just arrived."

In keeping with what was evidently the custom here, he looked me up and down. Obviously he tried to imagine my face hidden behind the veil. But he soon gave up.

"Okay. Go ahead."

We entered. The king was sitting on his throne, wearing the crown and royal mantle.

When I saw him, I went weak in the knees. My legs began to buckle, but the harem overseer held me up so I wouldn't fall.

What a beautiful man, God in heaven! Never before had I set eyes on such a beautiful man. A long face, carved out by a black beard (with a bit of salt and pepper), deep dark eyes, full mouth and lips, a nose slightly aquiline—enough to lend it a special charm. And his lordly build and his masculine aura . . . beautiful, beautiful.

I immediately fell in love with him. An overpowering, definitive love that, I was certain, would rule my life from then on. Blessed was the day he decided to call upon me. Blessed the letter he had sent me. Blessed his mouth that dictated the words in that letter, blessed the man, that beautiful man. I could spend years looking at him in mute adoration. I was finally discovering love. My little shepherd boy? Nah, he was just practice, training wheels. He had been but a warm-up for my next leap into love. And it was all within my grasp.

Solomon hadn't even noticed I was there, preoccupied with what I would later learn was his pet hobby; namely, passing judgment: deciding what was right and what was wrong, good and evil, deciding who was and was not justified. At that moment two women stood before him. Prostitutes, I immediately concluded. I had never seen harlots in my life; women like that did not exist in our village—and if they had ever dared to make an appearance, my father would have banished them, furiously shouting abomination! abomination! (or perhaps he would, for his personal pleasure, lock them up in a cave). But I didn't doubt for a second that those women were professional sex workers. The way they dressed, the gaudy makeup . . . whores, yes, indisputably whores. And ugly. Not as ugly as me, but ugly all the same, which made me suppose they were the off-brand, bottom-shelf variety. One-star prostitutes, at best. Maybe two, on a good day. Well, one star for the taller one, two for the shorter one, who had pretty eyes. At any rate, an average of, like, one-and-a-half stars. Okay, ranking them was not the point. The point was that there, in the presence of a powerful king, a wielder of divine mandate, were two prostitutes. Who felt perfectly at ease in the royal palace. Who spoke loudly and pointed at each other accusingly. After a brief shouting match, I finally understood what was happening: Each woman claimed to be the mother of a newborn that one of the guards held awkwardly in his lap. They had both given birth at the same time. One of the babies had died, but there had been a mix-up and, lo and behold, there they were, arguing over the child.

The whole thing weirded me out. So His Royal Highness, charged with the administration of a country, spent his time resolving quarrels between two women of ill repute? Solomon, however (but oh, man, was he good looking), couldn't have cared less about such objections. By the looks of it, prostitutes and other people of low class were regulars at the open house that his throne room periodically became. Plus, he obviously took pleasure in what he was doing. He listened to them attentively, asked three or four questions (irrelevant ones, in my view, but who am I to judge relevancy?). Afterward he went silent and meditated. And in that moment, I felt—and everyone there felt it, I think—that something was happening. Something had changed. The air grew dense, heavy, as if saturated with an invisible vapor. It was his wisdom. He exuded wisdom from his every pore and impregnated us with it. Which created a strange sensation, a prickly, funny feeling. One of the prostitutes, the one-star one, even scratched her thighs with her sharp fingernails. The whole thing served as foreshadowing of what was to come: his verdict. Which Solomon articulated in his deep, halting voice (God, his voice made me horny, my clit vibrated in unison with it). At first, his decision was shocking, cruel even: Since it was impossible to clarify who the true mother was, the child would be cut in half, each woman receiving one of the halves.

A shiver went down everyone's spine. The courtiers looked at each other, and I heard one of them mutter to the other beside him: "Our guy's playing fast and loose, he needs to rein it in—this won't go over well abroad." But Solomon looked confident. He immediately called over a soldier to fulfill his order. The man approached, sword in hand. A suspenseful moment, an extremely suspenseful moment, everyone frozen, holding their breath, a courtier covering his eyes with his hands.

One of the women, the two-star one, stood there in silence, as if resigned to the sentence, but the other reacted in an extraordinary way. She ran to the soldier, grabbed his arm, which was raised in the air, ready to strike, and in a strained voice cried, "If you're going to kill my child, I prefer you hand him over to her in one piece." A big uproar ensued. Then Solomon stood.

"Stop!" he ordered the soldier, who paused as if frozen in his tracks. He addressed the woman who had shouted, proclaiming: "You are the true mother. The cry we heard could only be that of a mother. He is your son. You may take him."

The soldier, a bit disappointed by the looks of it (his plans to slice and dice a baby that day had been thwarted), delivered the child to the woman while everyone cheered: clapping, crying, whistling, a real rave. The king smiled with satisfaction. He had something to be proud of: He had just provided concrete, palpable proof of his wisdom. Wisdom whose renown had spread throughout the world and transformed him into a living legend, into the monarch of monarchs.

It was in the presence of such a king that I found myself. Of course, I could have wondered if what I had just seen was, in fact, a demonstration of wisdom. And if the woman identified as the mother had gone mute with terror, what would the alleged proof of maternity have looked like? What recourse would she have then, except to go along with the sentence, allowing the soldier to cut the baby in two? Indeed, the barbaric act wouldn't resolve the issue; the king would still have to decide which half would go to which candidate. Even if the slicing had been done longways, there was no guarantee of symmetry. For example, the liver would end up on one side, the spleen on the other, not to mention both halves of the brain are not the same.

But that was nothing more than conjecture. The truth is that Solomon had knocked it out of the park, and in doing so had reaffirmed his reputation as a powerful and wise man, gifted—according to what was said in our village and many others—with supernatural powers: By sheer force of will he could instantly transport himself to any part of the world; he could talk to birds, which were the most agile and well-informed beings in creation; and thanks to his ring—his ring with four precious stones that I'd spotted from a distance—he controlled the force and direction of the winds. In the presence of that king, that man whose beauty bordered on unbearable, I found myself, me, his brand-new wife. Soon I would be nestled in his arms, soon I would bury my face in his chest, soon I would kiss that face, those lips, soon I would hear that voice whisper in my ear, "Come, my little bird; come to my love nest." There I was, waiting for the decisive moment, the moment that would cut my life in two, one half unimportant, hard and rough (an anomaly barely existing, already forgotten) like the rocks on the mountain, evidence of a life that had merely been a sad and out-of-tune prologue to a symphony of love, and the other, the true and radiant existence that would begin in . . . how many minutes? Ten, five, one?

Solomon was clearly a workaholic. It was his day for public hearings, and the throne room was full of people, mostly humble folk. In a smart move, he made a weekly concession to populism. He therefore spent the day resolving routine matters, family quarrels, property disputes, while I stood firm, waiting in my corner.

He finally finished waiting on people. He was visibly tired, and certainly irritated, which was no surprise given his exhausting schedule. Standing up with a groan, probably from back problems, he no longer looked so young. No one spends all day sitting around with impunity, even when sitting on a magnificent throne. He was about to leave when a courtier approached him and muttered something in his ear. His initial reaction, I noticed with a tightness in my chest, was of annoyance. Resigned annoyance, but annoyance.

"She's here? Today of all days, with all this commotion?"

He sighed.

"Never mind. Where's her file?"

My file? First my file? After all that waiting, me, his wife who had come all that way only to be put on hold, and the first thing he does is consult my file? For any other woman it would have come as a blow, a real soul-crushing blow, but ugly women have immense capacity for self-delusion, so I attempted to persuade myself that it must be standard procedure; seven hundred wives, three hundred concubines, it was within reason for him to obtain some prior information about the newest addition to his harem: name, age, filiation, place of origin, and so on. A sure indicator, however, that his married life had become a monotonous routine. At that moment I promised myself that it would be different with me: The monotony stopped here; with me, he would rediscover love. Let him get up to speed about me, let him memorize the standard dataset. But it would be his last appeal to systematized paperwork. Soon I would drag him through the tempest of my passion and his life would be made an electric shitstorm, a joyous insanity.

"The file!" shouted the courtier. "Quick, the king wants to see the newcomer's record!"

With surprising agility, from behind the throne jumped the old scribe I had spoken to earlier. The diligent little hobgoblin presented the scroll to the king: "Here is her file, my liege." Meanwhile, I was fortunate my veil hid my poorly contained anxiety as I waited there, standing but five meters from the throne.

With furrowed brow Solomon read the document. Evidently his problem was remembering: remembering why I was there, what treaty or transaction had brought me to the palace. It was no small task, by the looks of it; what he had in wisdom he lacked in memory. Perceiving what was going on, the courtier leaned over and muttered something more into Solomon's ear, upon which his face lit up.

"Oh yeah.... The daughter of that desert dweller... right, I formed an alliance with him. When was that, exactly? Like three years ago?"

His tone expressed surprise. Irritated but amused surprise.

"And he only just now got around to sending me the girl? After all this time? My God. I could accuse him of anything but being punctual."

Since they had to, the courtiers began to laugh. Satisfied with the success of his witty joke, Solomon, still on his throne, returned the scroll to his scribe and, ever smiling, turned to the wife he had just received—he turned to me.

The decisive moment had come, my legs turned to Jell-O and I started to shake and sweat, and I only avoided fainting because deep down I am, I think, very strong. He didn't notice any of it; nor did he seem interested; it was just one more marriage among many. He merely cast an inquisitive glance my way.

"Hey you, new wife, come here. I want to get a better look at you."

Mobilizing all my strength, I managed to take one step in his direction.

"Come closer," he insisted humorously. "I won't bite."

He laughed flirtatiously.

"Or better yet, yes I will, but not now."

The courtiers laughed, That's a good one, he's going to bite, but not now, nice, good one. As for me, I heard no evil, saw no evil. I only had eyes for that beautiful man. All I wanted at that moment was to fall into his arms and give him a wan look of passion. But he—obviously numbed by the bureaucratization of a matrimonial process more akin to an assembly line than anything else—was unaware of my passion. He examined me with a gaze that was not the gaze of a lover or fiancé, nor was it that of a seasoned husband. His was the gaze of an expert, a serial husband; what he was up to at that moment was assessing. To be clear, it wasn't like a farmer going to a county fair to assess livestock for purchase; no, it was too refined for that, and there was even a certain warmth in his eyes. But he assessed me anyway, looking me up and down. By the looks of it he wasn't put off by what he saw. She's got a nice bod, he must have thought. And I wished he would stop there, that he would limit his diagnosis to my curves. But then, almost in passing, he asked me to take off my veil.

Oh, why did he go and do that? Why? You're telling me the wisest of mortals, the man who speaks to birds, doesn't know there are some secrets that shouldn't be revealed, some veils that shouldn't be removed? Nothing would have stopped him from incorporating me into his harem with my veil in place, a decision that would confer a certain je ne sais quoi—and grandeur—to his collection of women: "This one here I call 'The Enigma' because I've never seen her face, but I love her all the same. I'm madly in love with her. I love her more than any other because true love is faceless and looks don't matter." But no, he had to give in to the vulgar temptation. Now that he had the goods, he wanted to examine them in toto, au grand complet. He stepped down from his kingly role to behave like a common shopkeeper. It really pissed me off. I felt like pummeling him with my balled fists, all the while screaming: "You ruined everything, dumbass, you think you're wise but you ain't shit!" But I couldn't do that. He was the king and I his obedient wife, just another obedient wife. With a brusque gesture I ripped off my veil and exposed my face.

He shuddered. Like the priest before who had examined me, he shuddered from fright—from fright, from horror, from everything. He couldn't help it—the expression on his face clearly transmitted what he was thinking, the same thing that everyone there was thinking: Good God, what on earth is that? A face? No way this woman was assigned to the royal harem, there must have been some mistake.

But he held it together. After all, nobody becomes a powerful monarch without some political acumen. He was in his court and had to preserve his image as an impartial ruler, balanced, someone above earthly matters, including the unfortunate face of a woman. Not a word escaped his lips, not one single comment. He settled on calling over the courtier. The two exchanged a few words in low voices. I couldn't hear them, but I could guess what they were saying. He being like: "This is absurd, how on earth could that man send me this creature? That's not a woman, it's an insult." The very embarrassed courtier like: "But she's the oldest daughter, the guy is just upholding his end of the deal."

He remained silent for a moment, frowning, his eyes lost. Finally, he turned to me. Without looking at me directly, visibly displeased, he excused himself for not receiving me in a more befitting manner—he was very fatigued—but I would be accommodated in the harem and the next day, or maybe in two or three days, depending on his schedule, he would send for me.

"What I mean to say is that you are welcome here," he recited, attempting to sound nice. "You are deserving of my affection, like my other wives, whom you will meet, by the way. They are many, but rest assured, there is a place for all in my heart. And a special place for you, of course."

In other words, the conventional speech which, up to that point, he had repeated so many times it was automatic. At any rate, he had fulfilled his obligation. He didn't hug or kiss me—there was no protocol for such moves—but he managed to send a smile my way, a half-hearted smile, the kind of smile torn between repulsion and a desire to please. Which wasn't surprising: Apparently, dividing was (Soldier, cut that baby in half) a formula that he regularly relied on for guaranteed success. Divide, conquer, repeat.

A courtier came forward and announced that the court hearings were over. Everyone bowed. King Solomon stood and with an almost unperceivable nod left through the side door, which led directly to his quarters.

For an instant all was silent. I looked at the courtiers. Some of them looked legit consternated. Others did a rather bad job of hiding their sadistic smiles. Meanwhile, there I stood, in my absurdly luxurious apparel, veil still in hand. What was I doing? What was I expecting? Finally, a courtier approached me and said that I ought to retire to the wives' chambers; surely I must be tired after such a long journey.

I lost interest, stopped paying attention. I was too busy staring at the throne.

Like everything in the palace, the throne was magnificent, made of gold and marble. It rested atop a staircase (twelve steps, one for each tribe of Israel) adorned with sculptures of lions. When the king was absent, their heads slowly moved up and down and side to side, as if warning those who happened upon it unannounced: This seat is taken, don't you dare covet it or you will be devoured. They were famous, those lions. Even back in the village people spoke of them: King Solomon's lions are going to eat you, was a common threat mothers issued to their disobedient children. People said that they were supernatural creatures, conjured by Solomon's magic. But they were little more than mechanical beasts, as I would come to find out. A servant, hidden in the basement, operated a set of gears to move them. In fact, the whole thing was designed by Solomon himself. Birdtalk he might not actually speak, but mechanical know-how, above all for mechanized illusionism, oh yeah, he knew his stuff.

I looked at the throne, my bitterness rising to the surface. And then, possessed by sudden rage, or perhaps despair, I impulsively climbed the stairs. But before I could reach the top, a courtier intercepted me and forced me down from them.

"Are you crazy, woman?" he yelled, furious. "Sitting on the king's throne, are you nuts?"

But that was exactly what I wanted, to sit on King Solomon's throne: a strange, farcical, and innocuous attempt to rise to power. However, it wasn't myself that I wanted to enthrone, but my ugliness. I wanted to flatter it, pay it homage, glorify it. I wanted my ugliness to be the one calling the shots. I wanted my ugliness to be the one passing judgment—Cut it in half!—I wanted my ugliness to be the one lecturing, the one pulling rules out of its ass. I wanted my ugliness to be the one reigning like Solomon reigned. I wanted my ugliness to be acknowledged, honored, worshiped. I wanted my ugliness to be so powerful that it would verge on beauty.

But my mini-coup was only part of my objective. Deep down, I wanted Solomon, I wanted my man. And, since I hadn't been able to hug and kiss him, I at least wanted to sit where he'd sat. I wanted to feel his leftover warmth there in the seat. I wanted the subtle emanation of it to penetrate me, to impregnate me, to inseminate me, if not literally at least metaphorically. It was Solomon's warmth; it was a part of his aura, his magic aura that irradiated out into distant lands; in that aura, in that warm atmosphere I wanted to abide forever, even if I had to dissolve myself in it. I would give up my individuality, yes, I would come undone molecule by molecule, as long as my molecules, aroused by Solomon's warmth, could vibrate in harmony with him.

The courtier, who wasn't even close to such complex aspirations, made me descend the staircase and delivered me to the harem overseer. Without further ceremony—at that point everyone there could already tell I wasn't a strong candidate to be the king's favorite—the woman grabbed me by the arm and took me, or better yet, dragged me along the corridors toward the wives' dormitory. The guards opened the doors.

"This is your new residence," said the woman, not without a degree of bitter irony. "Here you shall live out the rest of your days."

It was a vast hall decorated with curtains, canopies, and vases of flowers, all illuminated by torchlight. Dozens of comfortable beds were arranged in a row, numbered one through seven hundred (again, remarkable organization). All the women were already there, some of them lying down, others given over to the care of slaves, a number of them gathered together in groups, conversing. Everyone went silent as I, led by the overseer, advanced through the vast facility. Hostile silence, disdainful silence, ironic silence, befuddled silence, the kind of silence I was already used to. Beauty does the talking, beauty elicits enthusiastic exclamations from people. Ugliness shuts everything down.

"You're going to stay here," said the overseer, showing me to a bed. She looked at me, as if expecting some sort of complaint. At that point I had already changed my strategy: I would pretend that everything was going according to plan, that I was simply taking my place as Solomon's new wife. So much so that I began to praise the bed, yes, it was so big and comfortable. But then I spotted a pair of sandals on the marble floor. I asked whose they were.

"They belonged to the woman who used to sleep here," said the harem overseer in a casual tone. "She died, poor thing."

And with an ironic smile that expressed anger, the anger of someone who makes the beds but can't lie in them, she added: "Here in the harem one dies also."

That was the last straw, the culmination of bitter frustration. Why did I get a dead woman's bed? Why did I have to sleep where another had dreamed (and I knew exactly what she'd dreamed of: Solomon's body, his kisses)? Why should I have to inherit sharply shattered dreams, why should I have to cohabitate with finite memory, with the painful awareness of time rapidly going down the drain—without me ever having gained access to Solomon's arms? Why didn't they just go ahead and assign me a coffin or funerary urn? Why didn't they just put me out of my misery now?

I began to softly cry. The women, and I must recognize that they were sensitive in this, pretended not to notice. The harem overseer, hands on her hips, now observed me in silence. When I finally calmed down, she suggested it was time for her to go, but I stopped her. At the cost of losing her patience, she asked if I wanted something else.

Yes, I did. I wanted to know when the wedding would be. Her eyes went wide with surprise.

"Wedding? What wedding?"

"My wedding to Solomon," I stammered. "When will it be?"

She couldn't help but smile.

"But you're already married, dear. Your marriage was consummated the moment the scribe filled out the scroll with your info. You are now the king's wife."

So that was it: I was married. No ceremony, no banquet—but married. Had it been like that with the others? Probably not, surely some of the other marriages, or many of them, had been kicked off by a great feast, or at the very least brunch. But who was I to deserve a celebration? The ugly daughter of a distant village patriarch didn't justify investing so much effort, much less time and resources.

"From now on," the woman proceeded, "your routine will be that of all the wives. Thou shalt get up in the morning—early, because the king doesn't like lazy bitches—thou shalt work out to keep your body youthful and flexible. Next, a slave will come to wash you, comb your hair, dress you, get you all dolled up. And finally, thou shalt follow a strict diet—your meals will be rigorously regimented—and thou shalt remain in waiting."

"In waiting for what?"

There was angst in my question, angst that I could not and did not want to conceal, hoping that perhaps my angst would infect the woman, that she would share in a portion of my affliction, that she might console me, saying, "The king loves you, he has always loved you, always dreamed of you. You are the woman who appeared in his most splendid of visions; he knew of your existence long before you were born, better yet, he conjured you with his magic. From the four corners of the Earth he summoned the particles that would gather in your mother's uterus and give you life—he has been preparing you since the beginning to be the great love of his life."

But if she caught wind of the answer I so longed for, she played dumb. She was useless when it came to understanding and kindness. With a mix of astonishment and anger, she simply said: "What do you mean, waiting for what? Waiting for the king to call your number. You now live for the king, and only for the king. Nothing else matters."

She hinted that she needed to go, but I stopped her in one last desperate attempt.

"And when is he going to call me up?"

She shrugged.

"What do I know? No one knows, my dear. The king will send for you when he feels like it, when he remembers you. It could be tomorrow, it could be next week, it could be ten years from now. There are lots of you, got it? Seven hundred wives, three hundred more concubines, plus the occasional affairs... lots of you. Not even the king keeps tabs." She smiled. "He is very powerful, talks to birds... But at the end of the day he's just a man; you know how it is. His hard-ons aren't endless."

Again she tried to leave, again I stopped her, because this time my question was decisive; it represented the most crucial doubt I had ever experienced.

"Is it possible," distress rising in my chest, unbearable distress, "that he might never send for me?"

She thought for a few seconds. A few seconds in which she undoubtedly relished my suffering. And then she replied with an almost imperceptible smile, a very mischievous smile: "Hmm... I don't think that has ever happened. But it's not impossible. Especially since..."

She stopped herself. But I knew how the sentenced ended: especially since you're really ugly, and ugly women have an uncertain fate. That said, the woman wasn't a moron. I was the king's wife, and as such I held power, a tiny morsel of power, but power, and with my power she would not pick a fight. Gloating like she had gloated had its dangerous limits. It was best not to toy with me. If I, drunk with power, had jumped onto the throne, I could just as well, equally drunk with power, jump her. So she chose to encourage me. In a friendly tone of feigned solidarity, she leaned over and whispered: "Don't get too worked up, dear, the king will send for you."

She said goodnight and left. Right away a slave came to get me ready for bed. I tried to ask her questions, but she shook her head, unable to respond. Opening her mouth, she showed me why: They had cut out her tongue. Surely for talking too much, for giving away harem secrets. What happened in the harem stayed in the harem. In silence, the girl washed me, brushed me, undressed me, put me in a nightgown, tucked me into bed, and left. The torches were extinguished, the compound went totally dark.

Despite being very tired, I couldn't sleep. Because of the whispers and giggles and words spoken in hushed voices. Women chatting it up. Seated on their beds they exchanged opinions, traded viewpoints. And what did they talk about? Well, what else but the news of the day, the arrival of the newb? The ugly woman was the subject of all their ironic and aggressive comments: God, the king must have hit rock bottom to accept a woman like that. Well, I'll be, if I hadn't seen her for myself. There goes the harem, and to think that this was the greatest group of women in the Middle East.

I didn't get a wink of sleep all night. But then the sun began to rise, and I heard someone singing from a distance, some peasant woman off to milk the cows, and the song was so simple, so melodious, that it provoked real tears. Head buried in my pillow, I cried a lot, and then I felt better, ready to face my fate with resignation.

Just like the woman had said, there was little to do at the harem. We could eat, sleep, bathe, go on walks in the garden, a pretty garden with lots of flowers and bubbling fountains. Oh yeah, and we could converse, but no one talked to me; they kept giving me strange looks, the women. That's how my first day went. The king didn't send for me.

The next day he didn't send for me either. Or the third or fourth day. I began to worry—and to get irritated. What kind of crappy wedding was that, I wondered. After all, at the end of the day, it was a wedding. A wedding without ceremony, a pro forma wedding, a wedding that merely represented a ticket of admission to the royal consortium of wives, but a wedding all the same. I wasn't asking too much to demand that the king, my husband, fulfill his conjugal duties. True, I hoped for more than a fulfillment of duty; I hoped for more than a reasonable performance in bed; I hoped to live out moments of enchantment, of magic: an expectation multiplied by my naiveté and inexperience. What did I know of sex? Nothing. My entire past, in that sense, could be summed up by fantasies. As far as practice went, only my maneuvers with the stone—which I now remembered with considerable yearning. Our sex life, mine and my stone's, had been as satisfactory as possible. Perhaps I was dealing with volcanic rock and the lava from which it was formed contained miniscule fossil remains of mammals or reptiles or even insects, caught in the act of reproducing by the eruption, the final throbbing desire of their lives abruptly cut off and somehow preserved in mineral as a source of tenuous but constant libidinal energy; and that energy, mobilized and potentialized by rhythmic movement, had unleashed its rapid-fire orgasms that until then had constituted my only memorable experience sex-wise.

Solomon, beautiful Solomon, towering Solomon, with you surely it would be better than with my mysterious stone. When people spoke of his wisdom, I understood it as complete wisdom, encompassing all knowledge and all experiences in life; in other words, for me, it meant that in matters of sex he had completed his studies, with a bachelor's, a master's, and a doctorate. He had to be one of those initiates in the magical art of lovemaking, not just because of his extensive practice (seven hundred wives, three hundred concubines, a hell of a feat), but also because of the little birdies telling him things. Why else talk to birds, those unremitting travelers, if not for that reason? Along came a swallow to tell him, "Solomon, my dear, you have no idea what they're up to in the East, a little something called Kama Sutra, it's all the rage." Along came a raven to tell him, "I know a sorcerer who makes an aphrodisiacal potion that's out of this world, the bee's knees." That is, I imagined him not just as the king of Israel, but mainly as the king of the bedroom, the mightiest fuckboy in the known and maybe unknown world. I couldn't wait to get in the sack with him.

I wasn't alone in my burning expectation. I shared this sentiment, albeit begrudgingly, with all the other women. There in the harem the air was thick with anxiety, almost palpably so. Visible in frowns, in slack jaws, in assorted grimaces. Audible (especially at night) in moans, in sighs. And you could smell it in their chronic bad breath that stank up the air. The wives tried to neutralize their anxiety in a number of ways. Some of them sang in a choir, others danced, still others worked on their body language. But sometimes their anxiety rose to the surface in dramatic fashion. Women would get up in the middle of the night screaming their heads off as they ran between the beds like lunatics. They had to be restrained, tied down even. And the fights! It wasn't uncommon for them to wrestle each other to the ground, rolling around, hitting each other, biting, screaming with fury.

But were women not sent for? They were. Suddenly—it could even be in the middle of the night, frequently it was in the middle of the night—the harem overseer would show up, address one of them, mutter a few words in her ear or give the signal. Fingers crossed: After getting properly done up—there were maids and makeup artists on permanent retainer—the chosen one went on her way, exhibiting a radiant smile and distributing victorious looks left and right. But, and this was the big question, how had she been chosen, why had she been chosen?

There was no definitive way to forecast it. Not only was a wife-o-meter nonexistent (much less a gauge for concubines), but also nobody knew what led the king to choose this or that woman. As far as his process went, his intentions seemed as mysterious as Jehovah's; and perhaps that was exactly his intention: to become as powerful as a deity through unfathomable behavior. But he wasn't God. His desires were associated neither with omniscience nor with divine omnipotence. At the end of the day, he was just a man; a wise king, but a man all the same. Based on such reasoning, and after giving it much thought—time to think I had plenty of—I made a list of possible criteria for selection:

> (a) *physical attributes:* "Today I want one with olive skin, not very tall or short, with big breasts and wide hips..."
> (b) *psychological attributes:* "I would like an introvert. Not depressed, just reserved. The type who has deep thoughts and keeps secrets in her heart..."
> (c) *political factors:* "My alliance with that lesser king is crumbling. Bring me his daughter. In honor of her father, I'm going satisfy her..."

(d) artistic preferences: "Bring me that one who sings really well..."
(e) regionalist vision: "I want one from the South. It's been a while since I've been to those parts..."
(f) random choice: "Go in and bring me the first one you find..."

Needless to say, I had no one to discuss criteria with—much less with the king. Now, supposing he called on me and asked, "You there, new girl, what's your hot take on how I select women for my bed?" If that happened, I would have the chance to give an incredible exposition on the matter. There would be only one outcome: Confronted with my demonstration of intelligence, of culture, of wisdom even, he would exclaim, "What do I need criteria for? Fuck criteria, I've just found my beloved, a woman who is at my level; she shall be my life partner." In my dreams? You bet. But what else could I do except hold fast to a pipe dream?

The women did what they could to be called up. Most of them bet on appearance, which was constantly and diligently tweaked, dressing in the latest fashion being their prime directive. The harem was a real beauty mill. Slaves ran here and there with towels, basins, combs, mirrors, bottles of perfume, and creams. Women bathed, combed their hair, did their makeup, sprayed themselves with perfume, all the while shouting, "Brush here on top." "Put on more carmine." "Wipe off that shitty cream, I look dreadful, dreadful, dreadful." Dreadful, dreadful, dreadful? Did I hear that right? Yep: dreadful, dreadful, dreadful. But it was always rhetorical hyperbole born of some futile, tiny annoyance. Right here, I'm the dreadful one. Dreadful, dreadful, dreadful? That's me. And that's not to say I didn't put on makeup and wear perfume also. What else could I do? Sit around and bask in my ugliness? No. I tried. Even if just to pass the time, I tried to be pretty. With the quiet help of my long-suffering, mute slave, I tried. We gained very little ground (the poor girl would burst out in tears when she saw the scant results of our beautifying endeavors). My face would test the most competent of beauticians. But I tried anyway. Full-time, exclusive dedication, because the rule was: Be ready for the king's invitation. An absolutely imposing invitation: A summoned woman had to go, no matter what. Not even illness was an excuse, as I once found out: A woman who was in bed with a fever was sent for. She began to cry desperately: She had waited for this moment for so long, and now that her turn had come, she was sick, unable to tend to the king's desires, and to make matters worse, gaunt and out of sorts. But her pretext was rejected; the harem doctor showed up, examined the poor thing, gave her some medicine, and declared her able. It should be noted that, in her case, there were certain injunctions. The girl's father, a distant monarch, had challenged the king, who for his part, wanted to show who was on top, literally.

My time didn't come. The days came and went, but my time didn't come or go.

To kill time, I began to explore the palace—that is, the permitted areas, which, besides the harem and its garden, were two in number. One, a pavilion for sons and daughters: hundreds of children and teenagers there. According to the king's order, they had to remain separated. Up to a certain age, the mother could take care of the child. Later, she returned to her post as a woman on call 24/7, and the duty of child-rearing was left to the slaves and tutors. It was an enormous pavilion, even bigger than the harem's pavilion, yet more austere, without any decorations. A sad environment. Sad were the eyes of the children fixed on me. They suffered more than me, those kids. At least I had a father who had been present. A deadbeat, but present. What good came of being a miserable son or daughter of a powerful and wise king? Nothing. The king talked to birds, but not to his kids. True, he didn't talk because he didn't have time. Ruling a kingdom is absorbing work, exhausting, but the harsh consequence is that they felt like orphans. Orphans, but not blind ones. One time I tried to caress the face of a little kid and he didn't let me: "Don't touch me, ugly woman, don't touch me!" I left, furious—and sad. Even unhappiness triumphed over ugliness.

Equally depressing was my visit to the pavilion known as The Retreat. The old wives and concubines were taken there—"old" meaning women who had reached menopause (at least there was a criterion for it). The inhabitants of The Retreat were few in number. According to what I heard from a slave, they didn't last long after going there. Every day, they buried one. Now, not one of these women had been Solomon's wife or concubine, he being a relatively young man. No, the group was inherited from his father, King David. He'd promised to take care of them, which he did with some degree of dedication; he never came to the harem, but he did visit The Retreat regularly. Not to get laid, obviously, which would inevitably hint at an oedipal complex, but to converse and hear stories about a father who—and he of all people couldn't escape it—had been a distant figure, constantly about the Crown's business. The little old women, it should be said, liked his visits, which afforded them the pleasant opportunity to reminisce: "You father was a powerhouse fucker, my king. One time he fell in love with the wife of his officer, Uriah the Hittite . . ." and then Solomon had to hear the story of David and Bathsheba for the thousandth time.

If the emotional climate of the harem was anxiety, then melancholy prevailed at The Retreat. "We live off memories," the elderly women would sigh, "and those memories weren't always pleasant." All of them had passed through the royal bed at least once. For one, it was a glorious occasion, for another, pleasant; for a third, pleasant and glorious at the same time. Some of them, although few, remembered the moment with anger, with sadness, with disappointment; such was the case of the woman whom everyone there knew as the Senile Virgin. That was exactly her problem: She had never lost her virginity. The reasons why were obscure, especially since, being very old, you couldn't make heads or tails out of what she said anymore—hence the nickname. But whenever she referred to the matter, it was to complain: "Here I am, with my hymen turned to stone—who's going to do something about it?"

Stone hymen, stone phallus (wherefore art thou Stoneo?), misunderstood aspirations, bottled-up emotions, desires unfulfilled. Did fate have the same thing in store for me, for my virginity, to be or not to be destined for old age? The old woman was old, but not as ugly as me. Why, then, had she never had sexual relations? My diagnosis, based on stories that circulated about her, was prudishness. It seems that David had put a move on her, but he was vehemently rejected, with a lesson or two on morality thrown in—something David was very sensitive to, scolded as he'd been by the prophet Nathan for having coveted (and had his way with) his neighbor's wife.

I wasn't in the same boat. Prude I was not. Fortunately, the absence of horniness, associated with the absence of beauty, would reduce my chances with Solomon to zero in this climate of veiled yet ferocious competition. Fortunately, or unfortunately? Or was it precisely because of my limited possibilities with the king that giving him the cold shoulder would be a good approach, a lesser evil that might help me avoid a painful conflict?

An irrelevant question. The thing is that I was head over heels for Solomon, my thoughts were only of him, all I wanted was to sleep with him. The prospect of never having him, of dying without having kissed him, without having caressed his face, without having touched his body and without having been touched by his hands (he would play me like strings on a harp), the very thought of it saddened me, brought me to the brink of desperation. But I refused to hand myself over to desperation. I would fight until the end. I wasn't the type of woman who accepted her sad fate with resignation.

I decided to take the initiative: I would not leave it to chance, which certainly wasn't in my favor. If Mohammed refused to go to the mountain, then the mountain (with its lubricious cave) would come to Solomon.

To accomplish my objective I needed help, an assistant more efficient than my mute slave, as dedicated as she was useless. I had to get to the king. An alternative would be to resort to unofficial channels of communication; perhaps a courtier friend could whisper in the sovereign's ear, "Listen here, Solomon, the time has come to cut that ugly gal some slack. The poor thing doesn't sleep at night for thinking of you. Take her on as a charity case. Jehovah will compensate you—it'll look good on your résumé for the Final Judgment."

But there were two problems. In the first place, I didn't know any courtiers, and even if I did, I doubted they would be willing to intercede; the looks the courtiers had shot my way upon my arrival at the palace were filled with mockery more than with friendliness. And second, I wasn't after favors but rights. I wanted to stake my claim, not beg. Again, this would be difficult to accomplish alone. Who would help with such a task? And then it suddenly occurred to me: the women of the harem.

A patently absurd idea. If we were competing, and we were, why would they engage in a campaign on my behalf? And even if I got them on board, what would our campaign be?

I thought about it a lot during my walks through the gardens. Thinking, in fact, was something frowned upon by the harem overseer, who would get irritated every time she saw me wandering around the garden paths, head down. "You think too much," she would tell me, "that's why you're so ugly, because the ideas that pop up into your head make you furrow your brow and purse your lips, and the worry lines on your face are getting worse and worse. Relax, have fun, stay busy with silly but pleasant things and you'll see some improvement, at least a little—enough, maybe, to not scare off the king."

But I couldn't keep my brain from its machinations. And I was now plotting to mobilize the women. To get them to work for me? To get them to help me get into Solomon's bed? Yes, but not just that. I suddenly wanted more. I wanted solidarity, true solidarity of the oppressed. And I planned on sharing with them, in the most open and sincere way possible, my pain. I wanted to show them that my virginity was every little bit a part of their virginity (showing that even those who'd been deflowered continued psychologically and socially to be virgins), that my marginalization became their marginalization, that my ugliness was also their ugliness—if not an external ugliness, then at least internal, the sad and helpless kind, something along those lines. We had no reason to compete; on the contrary, only unity would make us strong and give meaning to our lives at the harem.

But how to go about it? To do so, I had plans. We would organize into groups to discuss the situations women faced in the harem, each group with its own coordinator and notetaker; we would hold a large assembly and, based on the resolutions determined by the assembly, I—the only literate one in the bunch—would write the Harem Charter, an impassioned document of protest against the conditions we lived in, which perhaps would clandestinely travel the world over, calling to action women imprisoned in harems everywhere. Rise up, victims of your sex! would be the cry of revolt that would echo from north to south, east to west, reverberating in the ears of rulers everywhere. The ultimate goal of the movement would not be to end the harem as an institution—many women wouldn't even know how to live free—but to at least establish a bill of rights. At the top of this bill I would put a minimum quota of fucks, to be determined scientifically: After studying the sexual performance of kings and sultans, an average would then be calculated to serve as the baseline. Another detail: Within the concept of a democratic sex life, each woman would have the right to the same number of nights in the royal bed. Arguments like, My dad's a powerful monarch and I deserve more, wouldn't fly. I'm prettier, I'm hornier—nothing of the sort. Now, there would be some margin for negotiation. If one woman wanted to spend a year fuckless, so be it. If a woman preferred another woman, in place of the king—cool. They could save up sexual credits to be used another time or traded for other types of gratification. Ten unused fucks could be redeemed for a tourist trip through the Mediterranean, on a comfortable ship, all expenses paid. If the king was economizing his sexual energy, nothing fairer than to compensate those who benefited him.

At the end of the day: a fine project, something capable of establishing a new paradigm of relations between men and women, at least in terms of the harem. Now: Was I being sincere in how I drew this up, or did I want to convince myself that I was a generous person, with a thorough vision of society and the world, a person capable of unfurling the flag of equity and justice into the wind? I didn't have an answer to that question. Maybe the movement was just a guise for my selfishness. And so what if it was? Was I an opportunist? Fine, so I was an opportunist. To the daring go the spoils, I told myself. Work smarter, not harder, and I for one am not going to sit here waiting for the king to get the hint to grace me with his attention. Whether out of idealism or for any other reason, I had to get the party started—waiting, obviously, for the right psychological moment.

It came sooner than I expected. Two weeks went by without the king sending for a single woman, which was uncommon. The harem became restless. Before rumors could begin circulating, with the help of the slaves I disseminated (even the one with the cut-out tongue joined in; she was very good at charades) my own version of events: The king had stated at court that he was sick of the women in his harem, some of them incompetent, of very limited sexual prowess. He must be thinking of creating a new harem, maybe in some distant place, like a tax haven, for example, where he could stash his money.

To my satisfaction, the story caught on. The entire harem was up in arms. It's an outrage, the women protested, for the guy to even consider such a thing. Who does he think he is? Not even a king can snub us like that. We try our best, we get dolled up, we put in the work, and the dude sits there, gloating, making fun of us, spreading lies to his jerk-off courtiers.

That is to say, my message spread like wildfire on a dry prairie, and now the flames of revolt rose vigorously. I took advantage of the moment and suggested a meeting. The first women I spoke to about it were afraid: Wouldn't that be an act of rebellion? I explained that it wouldn't: it was an orderly and peaceful demonstration. We had nothing to fear.

We met that very afternoon. Attendance was high. Roughly eighty percent of the wives showed up and fifty percent of the concubines (the latter feared conflict, due to their precarious situation). Wisely, I refused to preside over the assembly; I intended to talk, yes, but at the right moment. Debates and proposals ensued, without addressing the points of order, and in effect nothing concrete emerged. The moment arrived wherein the poor little things seemed to have lost the thread; they looked at each other and pouted, unsure of what to do or say. Now, I decided. As swift as a mountain goat I climbed the short wall of the babbling fountain in the middle of the harem and, with impassioned words (God, I was so inspired—nothing like long-repressed horniness to help channel eloquence), I called upon them to put an end to our abuse.

"Enough of being treated like sexual objects! Enough subservience, enough with the oppression!"

I took a deep breath and hit them with the slogan: "For complete equality of sexual rights! From now on the king will have to receive each of us!"

They erupted in applause. And then, having assessed the risk, and assessed well, I played my card. "And I will be the first one!"

A hush fell over the crowd. A tense hush. What I now saw on the faces before me was suspicion, not enthusiasm; distrust, not revolutionary fervor. And then from the back, formulated by a rawboned woman, came the one question I feared, but that I was sure would be asked at some point.

"You? Why you?"

I already had my answer prepared. "Because," I responded, "I'm ugly. If the king receives me, he won't have an excuse to refuse any of you."

Again, a hush fell. Many there—not all of them very bright—tried to understand my rationale. But an olive-skinned one with a crazy look in her eyes came to my aid.

"That's right! The ugly one is the test! Make the king receive her!"

The women now seemed mesmerized by the idea. Clapping their hands in unison, they shouted: "The ugly one! The ugly one! Make him sleep with the ugly one! The ugly one! The ugly one! Make him sleep with the ugly one!"

The ugly one? No. I was not the ugly one. At that moment I was not ugly. At that glorious moment, at that transcendent moment, at that blessed moment, for a fraction of a second, I had managed to see myself as if I were someone else. And what I saw was a woman standing on a wall, fist raised in the air, hair a mess, face—beautiful, yes, beautiful, very beautiful, of a different kind of beauty, but undoubtedly beautiful—glowing... Oh, if only that moment could extend into eternity, if only that beauty could last forever... They could call me ugly, yes, but they would be using the term in an endearing sense. Dearly ugly, adorably ugly, valiantly ugly, generously ugly. Beautifully ugly.

My ecstasy didn't last long. The next moment the overseer entered the harem, furious, and accompanied by staff members and soldiers.

"What the hell is all this shouting about? Where do you bunch of whores get off? Do you think the harem is a brothel, you pagan shitheads?"

A general stampede ensued. Despite my cries—"Resist, friends! United we stand, divided we fall"—they fled every which way. At the end, I was the only one left alone on the fountain wall.

"Get down from there," the woman commanded.

"No." I was bluffing, but I had to: What little I had achieved was in jeopardy. If they wanted to use force, then so be it. News of the incident would inevitably reach Solomon and could possibly help bolster my case—as long as I came out of it in one piece, but with soldiers, you never knew.

"I already told you, get down," she repeated, but now not so sure of herself.

"No. You're going to have to make me. But I warn you: It won't be easy, eh? It won't be easy. You'll never take me alive!"

My threat must have sounded pretty authentic, because she hesitated. Killing one of Solomon's wives, even the ugly one, even the rebellious one, could be considered a serious misstep. She changed her tune: "Stop fooling around, dear. Get down and we'll forget the whole thing."

"You stop fooling around. I'm only coming down for the king's bed. The longer he fails to fulfill his conjugal obligations to me, the longer I'm up here."

The overseer was now quite frankly alarmed. At that moment, a delegation of foreign rulers was staying at the palace. And if by chance they asked to see the harem? What would happen? What would they think when they saw a woman fit for a straitjacket, planted on the fountain wall, her ugliness aggravated by the ferocious expression on her face? It would be a terrible look for the kingdom whose image Solomon carefully cultivated. I had to be removed from there as soon as possible. And, since she couldn't get me down so easily, her only other option was to take it up with the king himself. A real pain in her ass. I mean, as overseer, she was supposed to avoid exactly this sort of thing—what happens in the harem stays in the harem. But without a doubt the alternative was worse, especially since at that point Solomon was probably already informed of the situation.

"Okay," she sighed, "I'm going to talk to the king. But do me one favor and get down from there."

"No way, José. Go talk to him and come back. Let's see how he reacts first, then I'll get down. Or not."

She looked at me angrily—besides being ugly, that one there is stubborn as a mule—but she went. And I stayed there waiting, the other women now watching me from a distance, in frightened expectation.

Two hours later the overseer returned. She now exhibited a dovish smile. "You may come down. The king is going to receive you this very night."

I confess that my legs were shaking. I had won, I had gotten what I wanted. The king was going to receive me, at long last, me. But it didn't make me happy or thrilled. Quite the opposite, I was terrified. At that moment I was but an ugly lady, very ugly, a shy little lady about to lose her virginity—oh, God. I became dizzy, but before I fell the overseer swooped in to help me down.

"Easy there, girl, easy. It's not a big deal. You'll see, everything will turn out all right. You'll live happily ever after." An ironic slight, served up as revenge. "Now come on, we have lots to do. I want you bathed and powdered. That way the king—"

She didn't finish her sentence, but I knew what would come next: That way the king won't think you're too ugly. Again, revolution burned within me. I shook her off.

"Leave me alone. You can keep your bath and powder. I'm going like this, as I am."

"But—"

"No buts. One way or another the king will have to accept me. If not, I'm going back up on my wall to take up screaming at the top of my lungs."

"Fine, okay, have it your way," she said, struggling to contain her rage. "But afterward, don't say I didn't warn you."

And she stormed off in a huff.

There were a few hours left before dusk. I tried to wait around on my feet, but I grew tired and ended up sitting against the wall. The sun completed its march across the Judean Desert and slowly disappeared behind the horizon. Velvety twilight invaded the harem. In a dialect that was unfamiliar to me, a handful of women began to chant to a nostalgic melody. Exhausted from the day's events, I fell asleep. And I dreamed. I dreamed I was back in my village, a child again and my father was opening his arms to me, saying with a smile, "Come here, my beautiful girl. Come." And I ran to him and was about to hug him, but in that instant someone shook me energetically, violently even: It was the harem overseer.

"Let's go. It's time."

Rudely awakened, I stood, still groggy. The woman looked at me with disgust.

"You're a mess, dear. A real mess. Much worse than usual. Let me at least show you."

She ordered someone to bring me a mirror. A good mirror, well polished, so as to leave no doubt regarding my likeness in its reflection. I contemplated myself with apprehension. And there were reasons for that: My reflection was simply dreadful. God, I was so ugly. My disheveled hair, my sleepy face—ugliness times two, at least. Noticing that I was visibly shaken, the harem overseer made one last attempt: "Do you want me to call for the makeup artist? Just five minutes—"

"No way." There was no going back now. "Let's do this."

We headed to the royal chambers, our footsteps echoing in unison along the empty corridors. I felt . . . How did I actually feel? Condemned. There I was, being escorted like a prisoner . . . en route to my wedding night. Marching into my husband's arms. Unbelievable.

We finally arrived, stopping at a large door guarded by armed soldiers.

"Wait here," the overseer said. In a low voice she exchanged a few words with the guards. They looked at me—the surprise on their faces was more than visible—and opened the door. The overseer let herself in. She returned a few minutes later, telling me to go in.

"From here on out, you're on your own," she told me, in a tone that barely hid her scorn. "Give it your best shot."

I didn't respond. I entered the king's chamber, trembling.

The first thing I saw was the bed. Enormous, with large silk canopies that reminded me, I don't know why, of a ship, something that I had never seen but imagined looking just like that. Well, there I was, about to board Solomon's ship. What was its destination? Would it set sail for the Island of Eternal Happiness, propelled by the sweet wind of love, or would it get lost in the billowy and dangerous Sea of Frustration? I couldn't tell. Ugly women are bad at guessing; they accept what fortune has in store for them.

Solomon wasn't there. Better yet, he was, but not in his bedchamber per se. Instead, he was out on the large terrace that opened to the entire region, illuminated in fantastic moonlight. With his back to me, he stared at the horizon. What could he be thinking? About new alliances with distant countries, about new wives to be incorporated into the harem? Or was he waiting to give his wanton bird of the night a few pointers for the sexual foray she was about to embark on?

For some time I remained there, waiting, watching that towering figure, his broad back, his beautiful head.

Then I got horny.

Can you believe it? Me, despite my tremendous anxiety, not knowing what would happen, the prick of desire welling within, growing stronger, and I felt that at any moment I was going to jump on his back and start kissing the nape of his neck . . . Before I could, he turned around. He looked at me and shuddered. Again he shuddered. I should have lost my shit; what's up with him shuddering every time he looks at me? But it had the opposite effect on me. I was now on the edge of my seat, so to speak, so much so that the fact that he shuddered only fed my desire, which was reaching unbearable levels.

He sighed. "So, today's the day," he said, with visible resignation. To buy some time, perhaps, he decided to strike up a conversation—but then he realized that he didn't remember my name, or who I was for that matter. I had to identify myself.

Him: "Right, how could I not remember you, you're such a striking figure." He wanted to know how my father was doing and my family and the village; in other words, he was making small talk, stalling, wasting energy—and worst of all, he was killing me softly. I couldn't take it anymore. Finally, he nodded toward the bed.

"Take off your clothes, make yourself comfortable, and give me one sec. I'll be right back."

The moment had come. I undressed in a flash and jumped into bed, covering myself with a sheet.

Big mistake. Unforced error. I missed the chance to show him my body, my nice breasts—in short, the best part of me, the part that could get his motor going.

Still hesitant, he was about to get in bed as well, but then changed his mind, saying he needed to meditate a bit more. "My responsibilities take their toll," he explained, by way of apology, and he went back out to the terrace.

It was too much meditation for my taste. I was hoping he would jump my bones, that we would roll around on the bed like a couple of lunatics and then fall to the floor. But no, he preferred his damn terrace. I felt like things weren't going to end well.

I had no other choice. When he finally lay down, with his silk robe still on, he looked like a man far from being overtaken with passion. He yawned, scratched himself, grabbed a glass of wine from his bedside table, took a sip, made a face (This wine is corked, I'll have to request a new bottle), and only then did he turn to me with the face of a kid forced to finish his homework: "Let's get on with it. Spread your legs."

Just like that: Let's get on with it, spread your legs. No words of affection, no caresses, no foreplay. Straight to the point, like a bartender who sleeps with a woman to indulge himself and right after falls asleep. But there were no limits to my fantasizing. It sounded to me like the sweetest of elegies, like a tender invitation to lovemaking. So, I spread my legs, and he got on top.

He got on top. But nothing happened. Wasn't I supposed to feel his hardware? Wasn't I supposed to scream with pleasure? Wasn't I supposed to descend into hell and afterward shoot up into the heavens like a ball of fire in paradisial orgasm? I didn't feel his cock at all, I didn't scream at all, I didn't descend or ascend even one little bit. Nothing went in my wet vagina. The awaited guest never showed up.

"Something isn't working right," he groaned, sweat beading up on his forehead. The anticlimax really irritated me. Was this how our supposed night of passion was to end, with a groan instead of shouts for joy? What was going on? I decided to investigate with my hand to see what the status was. Absolute disappointment: The circumcised royal cock was there, as I expected, but shrunken, flaccid. My act only irritated him.

"Who authorized you to stick your hand down there? Who do you think you are?"

"I'm your wife," I snapped back. "One more among many, but your wife all the same. You're my husband. And you're not getting the job done."

He remained silent for an instant, his eyes staring at the ceiling. Then he turned to me, at once hurt and furious. "Okay. You want to know? I lost my erection. It's never happened to me before, but now it did. I went limp. After seven hundred wives, three hundred concubines, and numerous flings, I went limp. Failure to launch. Mission aborted."

He scoffed. "And whose fault is it? It's yours. Who told you to be so ugly? Besides ugly, you're stupid. I'm going through a rough patch, faced with the threat of rebellion even. What do I expect from a wife in times like these? Understanding, patience. But no. You forced my hand, even staged a protest to make me receive you. And what did it get you? A limp dick. But you will bear the consequences and leave here the way you came, with your cherry intact. Bravo. It's the punishment you deserve."

It was the straw that broke my desperate camel's back. Sniffling and whimpering, "Don't do this to me, my king. Please, do not shame me." I latched onto him, kissing his chest, his stomach and then, out of my mind, following in my sister's footsteps with the shepherd boy in the cave, I attempted oral sex. Before he could get a word out, I fell face-first onto his pecker.

Dumb move. I was unaware, but I soon found out: A soft penis doesn't take well to fellatio. The resulting consequence was simply catastrophic. Upset, he jumped out of bed, stared me down, livid, and then pointed a shaking finger at the door: "Get out, abomination! Get out of here!"

Alarmed by the shouting, two guards came running in, spears at the ready—and there they stopped, bewildered, unsure of what to do. Which made him even more rabid: "Who told you idiots to come in? Did I happen to call for you?"

He came to his senses, realizing the risk he was running. If his guards spilled the beans about all this, his reputation would be forever tarnished. So he quickly put on a show: "My wife isn't feeling well. Accompany her to the harem and tell the overseer to take care of her."

Without resistance, I let them take me.

The women were all awake, obviously. Upon seeing me arrive even more of a hot mess than when I had left, and in tears, they knew what had happened. Their reaction was dignified: They could have made fun of me, they could have scolded me—Take a look at our dear leader, what a complete failure—but no, they said nothing, asked nothing. Two or three women helped me into bed, and one of them stayed with me, softly singing—a bit off-key but very emotive—so that I could fall asleep. Which only happened after a lot of crying.

The next day I was in such bad shape that I was unable to get out of bed. I spent the entire day crying, refusing to eat or drink. The women of the harem, sincerely dismayed, surrounded me, wanting to know what they could do for me. Maybe some fruit? Some flowers? Maybe singing would cheer me up?

But no, nothing cheered me up. Or rather, there was one thing that would snap me out of it—word from Solomon. If he sent for me, if he begged forgiveness for the whole fiasco—Forgive me, I was in a bad place but now I want to kiss and make up, I want to live out our love—oh yeah, if that happened, I would rise from my own ashes as a glorious phoenix and fly to him.

Solomon didn't send for me. Worse: In the following days he sent for others, several others. Not the merely pretty ones, but the prettiest. I got the message: Ugliness is a poison, ugliness is a real cockblocker—beauty is the antidote I need.

Intense anger began to grow inside me, a ruthless anger that took the place of my sadness. The bastard had treated me badly, like really badly. For example: What was the deal with him making fun of me and all? I was starting to think that Solomon was simply making excuses. A true man, a real chick magnet, would have got it on without concern for beauty—like, what difference did it make in the dark? Like, if the shepherd could smash a goat, then why would the king pass on an ugly woman? I bore the brunt of his failure. Which was, to put it mildly, profoundly unfair.

But it wouldn't stay that way. Gradually, I was coming up with a plan for vengeance.

He was the one who had given me the idea when he spoke of his worries about opposition to the throne. What he obviously feared most was a conspiracy against him. Therefore, that was exactly what I had to do: mount a conspiracy against him. Not to overthrow him—which would make me lose my status as a royal wife—but to get concessions out of him. In no time I was coming up with a daring and grandiose plan, so daring and so grandiose that I surprised even myself.

My plan was no more and no less than to kidnap Solomon. Kidnap him and demand as ransom, not jewels or money, but the fulfillment of his conjugal obligations to a scorned wife. Fuck or die. Or, at least, fuck or lose your balls.

Who would carry out such a plan? My father. My father and the people of our tribe. I knew they had been daring warriors in the past. In fact, for decades they had held back the invading royal army from subjugating them. They knew how to carry out surprise attacks and how to fall back before the adversary could recover. In their skirmishes my father proved to be a formidable commander and a great strategist, even if it was through trial and error. One of his talents, by the way, that I was now discovering I'd inherited from him.

Okay: What would my father get in exchange for participating in such a daring undertaking? Simple: He would recover his daughter's honor. He had never liked me, but he was the village patriarch and the type who wouldn't let someone who was flesh of his flesh, blood of his blood, be humiliated. And humiliation was just scratching the surface of the shitty time I'd spent in Solomon's bedchamber. It had been utter and complete humiliation, enough to decimate any woman's self-esteem, especially an ugly one's.

There was another angle to all this: Our marriage had not yet been consummated. Therefore the king could reverse it at any moment, which would mean taking back his support from my father. A risk that our joined flesh would avoid. That would be the desired outcome of my plot: Once kidnapped, Solomon would have to screw me or suffer the consequences. But the latter wasn't what I was after, especially since it would produce an unwanted outcome. I didn't want revenge. I was betting on an unexpected consequence (for Solomon, not me) of my politico-sexual attack. As I imagined it, Solomon would, at first, be afraid: Save me, my wife, please, save me from these people, these fanatical lunatics! Then I would say, Leave it to me. Gently I would lead him to a room. I would ask my father and his men to wait outside. Then I would close the door and say, Let's let bygones be bygones, my dear Solomon, let's start over.

In other words, in his moment of distress he would find safe harbor in my arms. I would be his protector, his wife and mother—what is a man but a forsaken child in search of motherly succor? The warmth of my body would be an unexpected comfort to him; he would be seized by warm feelings, followed by a firm erection—and then quite naturally we would be off to the races. And it wouldn't just be something transitory. He would forever remember that I had protected him like a shepherdess sheltering a threatened little goat. In the future, when he would find himself in a bind (and this would certainly happen often: threats from world powers, financial crises from excessive spending on the Temple and the like, physical ailments such as the threat of prostate cancer), he would turn to me, his friend and companion, his north star in the night sky, a safe harbor for the mastless ship of a man he would one day be. And then, with tears in his eyes, he would say the sincerest words of his life: I love you, Little Dove. (Little Dove: Yes, I had already determined what my pet name would be. Lions on his throne, Little Dove in his heart, that would be his life. He wouldn't need to talk to another bird again, only to his Little Dove.)

The details of the operation were already swirling in my head. I'd noticed that despite the palace's security precautions, it had its weak points. One of them was The Retreat, which wasn't far from Solomon's bedchambers. There were no soldiers stationed there. Clearly the chief of security had concluded it was unnecessary. Soldiers, what for? To nurse old women? The Retreat was, well, unprotected. And it faced an abandoned olive grove. A group of men determined to breach that stretch would have little difficulty in reaching the throne room and, after facing some resistance, take the king prisoner.

The next step was to inform my father. Tell him the whole story, ask for his help, and let him in on the plan. That part, paradoxically, seemed to be the toughest nut to crack. It wasn't simply a matter of our bad relationship; there was the problem of communication itself, of speaking with him. As a wife, and worse, the rebellious wife, I didn't have the slightest chance of leaving the palace. And no family visit was on the horizon for at least a year.

The way to go would be to send a letter. But how? Obviously, I couldn't go to the palace postal service. I began to come up with resourceful yet unrealistic ways to get the message to my father. Using, for example, a homing pigeon.

There was no lack of pigeons at the palace. There were thousands of them. Truth be told, they were a nuisance because of the filth they tracked in, but even so they were kept around and fed. It was Solomon's own doing. No one knew why he liked pigeons so much. It seems that his ability to talk to birds had led to a special relationship with pigeons, and more than once a servant maintained that they had seen him cooing melodically to them. On the other hand, members of the Columbidae family were symbols of love, attested to by a number of sentimental songs. Their presence, especially in the harem garden, constituted a delicate invitation to a loving marriage, and also a neutralizing counterbalance to the arrogant presence of peacocks that were there to reinforce his royal power against the sinister crows that sometimes appeared, cawing.

The pigeons in the garden were tame, and it wouldn't be hard to capture one. Now: How to train it? How do you transform it into an aerial messenger? How do you teach it the route to follow? An idea that occurred to me was to get the pigeon used to eating the fruit of a type of cactus that only existed near our village. Once conditioned to eating this fruit, it would have to fly in search of it and that way deliver the message. Well thought out, for sure, but how would I get the fruit of the cactus? I could request it from my people. But how? By homing pigeon?

There were other obstacles to consider. The message would have to be written on parchment. Which would be heavy for a bird of small stature because parchment was thick and dense. I would need several pigeons, at least, each one harnessed to a corner of the parchment, which means I would have to train them to fly in a squadron. In short, I apparently had an unsolvable problem. But then something incredible happened.

One day I was in the harem garden when I heard someone playing the flute on the other side of the wall. It was a familiar melody that made my heart skip a beat. I had only ever heard it in our village. I looked around and saw no one close by. I climbed the wall and saw that I wasn't wrong: It was the shepherd boy. There he was, the poor wretch, his face covered in scars, playing the flute and begging for alms. I won't deny that seeing him caused a flood of emotion to overcome me; I felt a lump in my throat, a tightening in my chest. Could it be a rekindling of our old flame? Maybe, but I didn't want to think about it. My man, the man I wanted to conquer, was Solomon.

I called down to him. Right off the bat he got scared. He even attempted to flee, but then he recognized me and waved at me effusively: "What a joy to talk to you, I knew you were at the harem, but I never imagined I would see you, they said no man can look at you now." He hesitated: might he be committing a transgression by talking to a wife of the king? I answered that our affection was above idiotic rules. First and foremost we were friends, and friends we would be forever.

He thanked me profusely: "You're very nice, and you have a big heart." He sighed: "I'm just so worthless."

"Enough of that," I said, "you made one mistake. It happens." And before he could get down on himself too much, I changed the subject, asking what he'd been up to since he left the village.

He shrugged. "Nothing worth mentioning."

He told me that after wandering for a long time, he'd made it to Jerusalem and decided to stay. Initially, thanks to a contact of his (I didn't want to get lost in the weeds of it, nor was I authorized to ask), he'd done okay, earned some money. But the fact was that he was currently out of work. He slept outside and lived as a beggar.

"It's hard," he said in a choked voice. "It's really hard."

He hesitated for a moment, then asked if I could help him get a little food—he had gone three days without eating. I felt bad for him, but immediately I realized that here was my big opportunity.

"I can do you one better," I said. "I can guarantee you good money." I paused, then added: "As long as you can do me a favor."

"What favor?" he said hopefully.

"I want you to take a letter to my father. He will pay you well for it."

"Your father?" He looked at me, clearly frightened. Which was understandable: he still bore the marks of the stoning. "But your dad wants to skin my hide ... because of my little escapade with your goddamned sister."

That last little bit surprised me, but it made sense. Surely he felt betrayed by my sister. She hadn't just refused to stick by his side in his disgrace, she'd swapped him out for another. But it wasn't the time to be talking about these things; I needed to convince him to deliver the message.

I insisted: "After my father sees what's in the letter, he will be very grateful to you. He might even reinstate you in the village."

His eyes shone. That was obviously what he most desired. He made up his mind instantly. "Okay, you can count on me. Where is this letter?"

I explained that I still had to write it. He was unaware of my ability; his eyes went wide: a woman who can write? Right then his esteem for me grew. I was no longer the patriarch's ugly daughter, I was educated—and to boot, a wife to the king. His admiration was obviously flattering, but I couldn't waste more time dillydallying. Someone might see me, which would really put me in a pickle. I asked him to return in three days.

"And how will you let me know?" he asked.

"You'll do the same thing you did today: play your flute. The same music. And I'll toss you the letter. Sound good?"

"Sounds good." After hesitating for a moment, he added: "I want you to know that I like you a lot."

Was that a declaration of love? And if it were love, had it blossomed in that moment? And if it had, should I encourage it? How? And to what end?

There were no answers to my questions. I was increasingly dying for romance, even a rushed one experienced from the top of a wall. Pump the breaks; I was already married, to a strange husband, but my husband, and that husband was who I was after, not the shepherd boy. I kept it short by saying that I also liked him, that I always thought of him fondly, and then I jumped down. In the nick of time: The harem overseer showed up right then for her usual inspection.

"What are you doing there?" she asked, intrigued, suspicious. I was now a person of interest, one to keep an eye on.

I played dumb, said something about getting some air in the garden. She looked at me with distrust—What is this ugly thing up to? She left the king flaccid, incited a rebellion and, if that weren't enough, here she is looking for more trouble—but she walked off without saying a word.

Nice. The whole messenger thing was taken care of. Now I needed to write the letter. But where would I get the necessary materials? It would be no walk in the park: only scribes were allowed such things, and they were a rare sighting. They worked in isolation in a closed-off room that only the king had access to. Even if I could speak to them, I would have a hard time asking them for parchment—it would come off as strange and draw attention, to say the least. And drawing attention was the last thing I wanted.

There was no other way, I had resort to bribery. With the only thing of value I had: a small bracelet made of gold and ivory (a present from my mom, not Solomon, who didn't give presents to any of his wives or concubines. He would be like, I don't want to show favoritism. Whether out of wisdom or greed, that was the rule). I paid off a guard, and he smuggled me a sheet of parchment, a quill, and ink.

One night, while everyone slept, I wrote the letter to my father by moonlight. And what a letter it was. Goddamn, was I inspired! I didn't stick to recent events. I went back in time: falling victim to Solomon's rejection was not an isolated event; rather, it was part of my natural history as the rejected ugly duckling—the expected consequence of the problematic relationship between a distant, authoritarian father and his sensitive and bitter daughter. I spoke of that girl's angst and aspirations, of her hope invested in the affection of the man she'd been destined to marry. In scathing terms I described the humiliation she had gone through, and that it extended to her family, compromising the entire family tree, all the way to the tiniest twig. I wrapped it up asking my father, in the name of our ancestors, to help me. After the long and eloquent introduction, I went on to more practical issues, explaining in minute details what he had to do to break into the palace and kidnap the king.

I ended the letter on the same day the shepherd boy was to stop by the palace. He kept his promise. At the arranged time, I heard the sound of his flute. I ran to the garden and tossed the scroll over the wall. The die had been cast. For the first time in a long time, I prayed: I asked Jehovah to help me, to get the message to its destination. I felt calm afterward, consoled. I'd done what I set out to do. Now, I only had to wait.

And then, a surprise.

Around dusk, the harem overseer came looking for me: "The king sent for you."

I couldn't believe my ears. The king, sending for me? The king, who days before had banished me from his chambers? The king, who had rejected me in the most thoroughly grating way possible? Perplexed, I didn't know what to think. Had Solomon finally decided to yield and fulfill his obligations? Perhaps: His legitimacy as monarch, the future treaties yet to be celebrated, depended largely on his marital performance. Maybe he had taken precautions against the risk of another failure. Example: aphrodisiacs. Example: an orgy—during which, lusting after the other women, he would kill two birds with one stone by throwing me into the mix.

There was a second possibility, but it came down to a flat-out miracle: Had he suddenly realized that what he felt for me was, in reality, love? Could he be sending for me to tell me that the memory of my hand, or that of my body (but not my face), had worked in him like a magic filter of passion, although with a delayed response?

And, finally, there was a third possibility. Dark yet not inconsistent with royalty's Machiavellianism. Could Solomon have commissioned the burden of deflowering me to some third party, the completion of his mission a state secret? A humiliating hypothesis, but at this point I would take a vicarious, transitory husband, as long as he was substituted in due time by dear Solomon. The sacrifice would be worth it then.

At any rate, one thing was certain: I had acted rashly in sending my father the letter, and I had been rash in asking the shepherd boy to be my supporting mailboy. Worst of all, the guy was already on his way, eager to fulfill his mission, a mission that he imagined would help him extend an olive branch to my dad. I needed to stop him, but how? Go after him, me? No, I couldn't do that, and it would be pointless anyway. I would never reach him in time. The best thing to do was to go to the king, immediately. If everything turned out in my favor (in other words, a steamy sexcapade with him or someone designated by him), I would confess what happened, ask him to forgive me and to help me stamp out my father's catastrophic attack. Wise as he was, Solomon would understand. He would send his swift horsemen after the shepherd boy. The message intercepted, the shepherd boy would receive many goats for his troubles; all's well that ends well, and we would live happily ever after.

With this brilliant prospect in sight, I quickly dressed and ordered the makeup artist to make haste.

"No need," the overseer cut me off. "You won't need it today."

"What do you mean I won't need it?"—me, perplexed—"But the king..."

"The king said it won't be necessary. Let's go. You don't want to keep the king waiting."

Again I marched down the long and gloomy corridors—but, surprise, surprise, not toward the royal chambers. Instead, we went to the throne room, which immediately had me intrigued, and worried.

"Why are we going this way?" I asked the harem overseer.

"That's for you to find out," she said. And then she left me waiting alone at the doors.

Two courtiers showed me in. There was the king, sitting on his throne. Upon seeing him, I almost fainted: he had a scroll in his hand. My scroll. The letter I had written to my father.

I didn't know what to do. Should I grovel at his feet and ask forgiveness? Should I explain, It's not what Your Majesty thinks, it's nothing more than a joke, a game between father and daughter? But words wouldn't come and I stood there frozen with courtiers on both sides. As for the king, he went for a fixated, inquiring glower. The silence in the room was unbearable. It was threatening.

"I just intercepted your correspondence," he finally said, in an absolutely neutral tone. "A crappy thing to do on my part, I recognize, but since you didn't use the palace postal service, I felt authorized to do so. Furthermore, you have to agree that the matter involved the security of the kingdom. So, I sort of had to do it."

Despite my panic, it wasn't hard to re-create what had happened. In the same moment I threw the letter over the wall, the shepherd boy was being detained by palace guards. They were interrogating him when something unusual fell from heaven, so to speak. A rolled-up piece of parchment tied with a bow. The guards then delivered it to their commanding officer who, suspecting something was afoot, took it to the king.

"Conspiracy against the throne," Solomon continued, "is no laughing matter. You know I can condemn you to death, right?"

Of course I knew. For much less my father had stoned the shepherd boy. The law was severe in our land, very severe. An eye for an eye, tooth for a tooth. But if he thought I would throw myself to the floor, crying and begging for forgiveness, well, he had another thing coming. I'd had my fill of humiliation. He could go ahead and have me killed; it was within his power. But I would die with my lips sealed and dignity intact.

He did not, however, have an execution in mind. There was nothing threatening about the look he was giving me. Au contraire, he seemed to think the whole situation was funny. And it was putting ideas in his head, as I would soon find out.

He asked his courtiers and soldiers to leave us. He stood, descended the steps of his throne and, leading me to a divan, asked me to sit with him. Again he looked at the parchment.

"It's very well composed. Enough to make any scribe green with envy."

He looked at me intently. "Did someone write it for you?"

The question put me on the defensive. He must be looking for clues to a palace-wide conspiracy. In any case, I wasn't about to lie. I said no, that I had known how to read and write for some time.

"Amazing. You are the first learned woman I've met," he affirmed with an admiration that, I'll confess, massaged my ego. It was a poor substitute for an erotic massage, but given the circumstances, I was in no position to negotiate.

"If that wasn't enough," he continued, "you write very well. I couldn't stop reading. And look, I'm no bookworm. My wisdom comes from meditation, not books. And from what birds teach me."

Surprising praise, which I thanked him for, now only partially suspicious—too much alms for the poor saint that I was. There must be something behind it all? There had to be.

"I want to make you an offer," he said. "But before I do, let me ask you a question. You know the temple I built? The Temple of Jerusalem?"

Yes, I knew the Temple—from the outside, since going in was something forbidden to women. That giant, opulent edifice didn't impress me much. But he, on the other hand, considered it the great achievement of his reign. And then he began to talk about the Temple. It wasn't about a dream that was his, but an old dream that belonged to generations that had come before him. And it had fallen on his shoulders to turn it into a reality. In effect, he'd spared no expense in search of gold and the finest wood. His ships had crossed oceans to faraway lands populated by bronze men who walked about naked, adorned with feathers, and who spoke an unknown language. Thousands of workers had been mobilized, immense quantities of riches spent, but after thirteen years the Temple was practically ready, bearing witness to God's presence and standing as a symbol of religious unity. Pilgrims now came from all over the country to pray and offer sacrifices there. Jerusalem had become a sacred city, as well as the political capital. All of which he considered a personal success, a consecration. True, he'd had a huge leg up, thanks to the idea of one god. The prohibition of idols had helped a lot, because each idol is an expression of a group and each group has its own interests. The Temple represented the overcoming of tribal interests; it conveyed national unity.

"But," he pondered, with a level of sadness. "It is a physical feat, a material thing. I hope it stands the test of time for many centuries, but who can guarantee such will be the case? Who can guarantee it won't be destroyed? I don't want to be remembered for ruins. I want to be remembered for something that lasts forever, you know?"

He paused, looked at me, and solemnly said: "A book. A book that tells the history of humanity, of our people. A book that will be the cornerstone of our civilization. Of course, as an object, books are also perishable. But what's inside books is not. A message that can be passed down from generation to generation, something that sticks in people's minds. And that spreads throughout the world. Books are dynamic. Books disseminate like seeds in the wind."

He took my hand—OMG, he took my hand, my beloved took my hand. It was finally happening, oh, God, God, make him say to me now—now!—that he loves me. Please make him, God. Tough luck:

"I want you to write that book. I want you to describe the trajectory of our people through time. I want you to speak of our patriarchs, of our prophets, our kings, our women. I want a lovely narrative as well written as that letter you sent your father. I want a book that generations to come will read with respect, but also with wonder."

I was shocked, to say the least.

A book? That was what he wanted from me? A book? You mean he didn't want to take me to bed? He didn't want to make love? He wanted a book? His proposal awoke within me contradictory feelings. On the one hand, more disappointment. Instead of a declaration of love, a book proposal. On the other hand, all things considered, I felt flattered by his choice—proof that he recognized I had worth. It wasn't the worth I most cherished; I wanted him to find worth in me as a woman, as a lover. I had yet to obtain that. Patience. In any event, it was progress, extraordinary progress: from scorned—no, from almost condemned—to the status of collaborator. Which put me in a unique position. From then on, one way or another, I would be at his side, the wise king and his intellectual wife.

Okay: to write what he was asking for was a gigantic undertaking. I didn't have the slightest clue how to go about it, I didn't even know where to start. Sudden discouragement—not to mention terror—hit me like a brick. I realized the chance of failure was high. And one failure—one more failure—was something I couldn't afford. Failure as a writer, failure as a wife, failure as a woman—was that all life had in store for me? Why couldn't life just leave me in peace?

There I was, minding my own business, holed up on the mountain, just me and my ugliness and my stone; for what purpose had I been dragged down from there? To suffer in disillusionment? To face a challenge greater than my modest strength?

Apparently unaware of how torn I felt, Solomon plowed on: "Don't go thinking this is a personal promotion. As far as I'm concerned, nothing more than a chapter, and it can even be a short chapter. Simple, abridged. Of course, the building of the Temple has to be in it, in detail. But you don't have to mention that I talk to birds. Tradition will take care of preserving that. Just talk about my works, about my passion for wisdom." He looked at me. "Did you hear me? Are you paying attention to what I'm saying?"

I told him yes, that I was listening and paying attention.

"You seem a bit distracted," he observed somewhat sourly. "I want to remind you that we are talking about a mission. And I want to remind you that there is a pending accusation against you."

He caught his mistake: If he wanted my help, he wouldn't get it with reprimands and threats.

"You might ask," he went on in a more conciliatory tone, "why I'm soliciting your collaboration. Impossible, you might say, that such a powerful king has no one to write the book he so desires. And I might answer: Well, I tried. You have no idea how hard."

He interrupted himself. "Come with me. I want to show you something."

We crossed the throne room and came to a small door that was partially hidden by a curtain. It opened into a vast room that smelled musty. From the ceiling to the floor there were shelves full of manuscripts and, sitting around a large table, six ancient-looking men with long white beards. No sooner did we enter than they stood up, casting me a look of offended astonishment: Women were unwelcome in a place that was obviously the palace's stronghold of knowledge. But the king was there, and that was what mattered. They approached him and, ignoring my presence, all began to talk at once in an incomprehensible and intolerable cacophony of gibberish.

Solomon asked them to calm down. "All right, gentlemen, all right. At a later time we shall discuss each of your concerns."

We left. He closed the door behind us and turned to me with a dejected smile.

"See? Those are the men I placed in charge of the whole operation. They've been at it for more than ten years. They talk and talk and talk and write and write and write—and get nothing done. They know all they need to know, but they quarrel so much that they never reach an agreement about the final text. That's why I sent for you. In the first place, you're nothing like them: you're a woman, intelligent and keen. Then there's the fact that you write much better than all of them put together. Your letter is proof of that. I read it at least three times."

He remembered something that made him laugh with amusement.

"The part where you describe me as an insensitive husband . . . That was really good. You almost convinced me that I really am the villain. By conferring this mission on you, I count myself rehabilitated."

Good God, he might be impotent, but he was a prick-eared fox; oh yeah, that he was. With his praise, I was putty in his hands. But I managed to maintain my cold-bloodedness; more than that, I too was, modesty aside, cunning, as cunning as he was. I could have said, I'll do the book if you take me to Poundtown. But it wasn't the right time to go demanding as much, what with how blatantly raunchy it sounded. When I finished the job, when I took him the final draft, saying, Here you go, Solomon, your literary temple, he would be unable to resist falling into my arms. I would not only be his lettered wife, I would be, in deed and by right, his queen.

As impressed as I was with my own cleverness, however, I began to have doubts. Between the two of us, who was pulling one over on the other? A more pressing matter; when it was all said and done, I was dealing with the wisest man among mortals, the man who knew everything about duck-billed platypuses and how to communicate in birdtalk.

But I wasn't interested in competing in a battle of wits. Especially since his proposal had worked in seducing me, just like his liquid black eyes had seduced me. Writing his book wouldn't just be his achievement, it would be my achievement also. I would never have to build a temple; but the work he had in mind for me, yes, that was within my reach, even if it took me a lifetime to write it. We were in this together, he and I. If we didn't share a bed, at least we would share a common goal. We would take shelter in the text, alone together, far from his seven hundred wives and three hundred concubines, far from his throne and its lions, far from the pigeons that shit all over everything, far from political intrigues and public audiences. To be honest, the prospect of writing the book seemed so exciting to me now that I felt rewarded by the simple idea of being involved in it, of following the narrative thread like someone following clues in a labyrinth. In the unknown territory I was about to explore, maybe I could set out with the same resourcefulness I had developed while alone on the mountain trails. Now: what if along the way I found a cave . . . and what if Don Solomon wanted to join me in the cave . . .

The cards were on the table (there were, of course, cards up sleeves too, multiple cards up multiple sleeves, but those cards were to be played much later). And I had already made up my mind.

So when he asked, with his habitual niceness, whether I accepted taking part in the enterprise, I didn't hesitate: "Deal," I said. And I added, a bit hastily: "If possible, I can get started now."

He smiled—I knew at that moment he didn't see me as so very ugly, that he had discovered in me a hidden beauty, the beauty of intelligence and culture.

"I knew I could count on you. I'm going to tell the elders that, from now on, you are officially a writer. Your work begins tomorrow."

The king wasn't fooling around. The next day, I was brought to a room prepared specifically for me. There I would reside until I finished the work. As he explained it, he didn't want me distracted by harem gossip. Additionally, my job would be kept a secret until I finished. Among other reasons, because he was worried about plagiarizers and the ways they could use the text. A leader from the opposition who went public as the author of a monumental history of our people would garner immediate attention and respect that would turn him into a dangerous adversary. A testament to his wisdom, Solomon feared the pen more than the sword.

It was a large place, my room. In addition to the bed and wardrobes, there was an enormous table, chairs, and shelves full of manuscripts, which had been transferred from the elders' study that morning. Solomon's actions sent a clear message to his staff: There's a new girl on the block, amigos; adapt or perish.

On the table, writing utensils, including new parchment. I smelled it: goatskin. The poor thing had been sacrificed so that the letters dancing around in my head could be transformed into visible signs, into words. Those letters, laid out line after line, would mark the path that would lead me to victory—and to the king's heart. Blessed parchment. I could see my future in that virgin surface, a glorious and breathtaking future.

I spent that day, and the following days, revising the materials that the elders had collected. The king was right: it was a jumbled mess of legends, historical events, religious precepts, all very poorly written, and with spelling errors. As sources of information they were fine, but for the book that Solomon wanted, I would have to start from scratch. When I came to that realization, my confidence wavered once again. The immensity of the task came crashing down on me; suddenly, I was no longer a confident, self-assured woman, but a helpless little girl. All I wanted was for my mom to rock me in her arms like she did when I was a child with fever. I set the scrolls aside and lay down, devastated.

But no, I refused to let myself get discouraged. I had to overcome the inertia, that gray melancholy that threatened to overpower me and take me prisoner forever. I had a story to tell—a big story to tell—and I was going to tell it. I jumped out of bed as if propelled, returned to the table, brandished the quill. Yet I hesitated. Where to even begin? I closed my eyes—and in that instant I saw it. Before me an immense figure, indefinite, an immovable diaphanous presence above an infinite, dark ocean. That was all I saw, but it was enough. In the fraction of a second that my vision lasted, I could feel the tension built up for all eternity in that remote figure: the tension of the conceived universe, not yet created, the tension of frozen time, ready to run its course. Somehow an infinitesimal fraction of that incalculable energy was transmitted to me. It was enough. I dipped my quill in the ink and wrote: "In the beginning."

And there I stopped, already unsure of how to continue. Mystery had cast its shadow between tension and action. The beginning—what had even happened in the beginning? My head was hollow, empty; I couldn't remember anything I had read in the piles of manuscripts; the words I had written seemed to me an enigma more than anything. Then I let my gaze wander, and I no longer looked at the letters but at the parchment, with its granular surface.

The parchment. It was from there that I should set out to explore our origins, from the skin of an animal sacrificed so that one day I could write on it. The skin; before the skin, the goat; before the goat, the leaves it chewed on; before the leaves, the tree, the Earth, the universe. I needed to reconstruct that history, what it meant to go back centuries and millennia in time, dive headfirst into the cosmic maelstrom that would take me . . . where? Shit, I didn't have a clue, and with surprising swiftness that question drove me to insanity, but not like everyday insanity, I'm talking the existential kind, a very serious issue, more suited for a philosopher than ugly little me. What to do? Let's start with God himself, I thought desperately, and that was an enormous relief. God: now that was an idea I could work with. No: an idea I could dissolve myself into, more completely than salt dissolves into water. The bleating goat of the past, the goatskin that stood as my accuser in the present. I was starting with God. Why God and not Goddess? Why Jehovah and not Astarte, the divinity that other people in the region worshipped? Why a beard and not a smooth face, with a few moles at least, or maybe a lot of moles? Because of one simple and definitive reason: I couldn't begin the great book with an affair, especially when considering my patron. Solomon spoke of God, the elders spoke of God, my father spoke of God. God! shouted the mountain. God! shouted the birds, from songbirds to flightless ones. Ergo, God. In my head, God was but a generative energy, not an anthropomorphic figure who reigns over his creation. That Solomon & Company imagined him as a man mattered little to me. I would express my disbelief, and my protest, by abstaining from any description of divinity. That they imagined him as an old man with a white beard and a stern look meant nothing to me.

"In the beginning God created the heavens and the earth." Nailed it. Once written down, the sentence sent a sudden wave of euphoria through my body. I began to laugh. I laughed so hard that one of the elders—they were in their study next door—came to see what was going on. He entered without knocking and found me sitting there at the table, quill in hand, parchment in front of me. It served him right, witnessing what was, in his eyes, an abomination: I was writing the history that up to then had exclusively belonged to the elders. Unable to hold it in, he let out a hateful cry and ran off.

What did I care? With my task well under way, I was now ahead in the game. "God said, let there be light, and there was light." Awesome, now we had light—and darkness too, because you can't have luminosity without shadow and shade. In the following paragraphs the plants were created, and the stars, and the fishes and the birds. . . . All very quickly, which on the one hand was good—I was making progress with considerable speed—but on the other hand I didn't like it. I would prefer more details. How did God create lettuce? And piranhas? I would like to describe God manufacturing any one fish, choosing its scales, choosing its fins, saying, Hmm, the shape of its head is off, the tail could be bigger. But let's be real: at that point we would be talking more of a cabinet of curiosities than a sacred text. Summarization was essential for instilling awe. Besides, I didn't have all the time in the world. Given the magnitude of the task at hand, I needed to move quickly. I summed up the creation in six days, included a seventh for rest, making it clear that haste wasn't an enemy of perfection: "And God saw everything that he had made, and behold, it was very good." I didn't want to put "great," or "excellent," or "wonderful," because in the end, even Mr. All-Powerful ought to be a little modest. Let's say that on a scale of one to ten he gives himself an eight, his imperfection on account of reptiles and ugliness.

The introduction was easy. But I foresaw difficulties ahead. At issue was the creation of the first man and woman. The elders had piles of scrolls written on the subject—bland, monotonous reading, which I quickly abandoned. In terms of man and woman, of masculine and feminine, I would simply let my instinct do the talking. And letting my instinct do the talking was easy.

According to the elders, God had created the first man from clay. I had no objection to that humble raw material. But why the man first and not the woman? And why had the woman been created differently? To put it lightly, the story about the rib struck me as idiotic, an affront even, considering the simplicity of that body part.

I decided to correct such mistakes by mobilizing my own imagination. Once created, the first man and first woman fall madly in love with each other, and then they transform Eden into a stage for their rapturous lovemaking. They fuck left and right, on the grass, on the sand, in the shade of trees, on riverbanks. They fuck ceaselessly, as if all of eternity preceding creation contained nothing more than their passion in the form of highly concentrated energy. Their encounter was thus a sort of Big Bang of sex, very Big and lots of Banging. They did it in every position and experimented with every technique, all under the wide-eyed gaze of goats and duck-billed platypuses and, lest we forget, under the benevolent watch of God.

Which, in my version, didn't get them kicked out of Paradise; quite the opposite, he encouraged them: Now that ye know love, ye can face life for what it is, life full of sound and fury.

I finished the chapter and reread it. It was really good, so good that I started to have doubts: Was it really a historical text? Wasn't I just transmitting a message to Solomon? Something like, Lookee here, Limp Dick, stick to the script and know that she who is hot on the page is a freak in the sheets. Could it be that I was hoping to turn him on? I tried to convince myself that I wasn't, that I was simply caught up in the thrill of a story about two lovers in Paradise—but I took the scroll to the king not without certain worry, and expectation.

Solomon read it in silence. Afterward he set the manuscript aside and sat there reflecting for a few moments, his eyes lost. Confirming my deepest fears, my version troubled him. Which he chose to put on hold.

"I don't know," he said, finally. "I'm going to have to think about what you wrote."

He paused, then added: "And I also want to hear what the elders think of it. After all, they are the repositories of knowledge about our past."

Blood pounded in my ears.

"Listen, Solomon," I said, forcing myself to remain calm. "If you're going to take their word for it, we're wasting time. Those guys will never approve. They—"

I was going to say that they were nothing more than a band of nincompoops, but I held back: You don't talk about rope in a hanged man's house. "They have a different narrative style, you know?"

Again he resorted to diplomacy. "I know, I know. But let's see if we can find a middle ground for everyone. Especially since the elders have some sway. They were all handpicked by the high priests of the Temple, you know, and when it comes to the clergy, you can never be too careful."

There was nothing more to say. I said goodbye, asking him to notify me as soon as he had it worked out.

I returned to my room and went to bed. Restless, I couldn't sleep. Right when I was finally starting to drift off, someone knocked on my door. They were not the energetic knocks of the guards or the harem overseer. No, they were timid, furtive knocks, which left me more intrigued than scared: Who could it be at this time of night? Solomon? Solomon who, having finally discovered his love for me, had come to my bed for our much-awaited wedding night? Fat chance. Solomon didn't need to knock on my door. He was the master, master of the palace, of women, of everything. But, if it wasn't Solomon, it could only be some lame-ass nobody. Annoyed, I got up, lamp in hand, and went to answer.

Before me stood an elder, one of the six bearded gnomes appointed to guide my hand in the art of the written word. I didn't know his name; in fact, I didn't know any of their names; they were all the same to me, a bunch of wrinkled clones. Why had he strayed from the group? Why was he at my door, a toothy grin on his idiotic face, stammering an apology for the inappropriate hour?

"I'm here about your work" he said, showing me the parchment, my parchment, the parchment I had worked on. "You know, the work that the king has entrusted us with."

Entrusted us with. We were already coworkers. Which was some sort of progress. By the looks of it, mistrust was giving way to partnership, even if at an ungodly hour.

"I was up reading your text," he continued. "It's good, very good. But I think some details should be, in my opinion, discussed . . . By the way, can I come in? I know it's late, but this is an important matter . . ."

Okay, now he was weirding me out. Discuss the text, at this time of night? There was something fishy going on. I thought it best to cut the chitchat.

"Can't it wait until tomorrow? To tell you the truth, I'm kind of tired."

"Please," his tone was now pleading. "It's that I . . . I'm afraid I'll forget . . . it happens, you know . . ."

If he was afraid of forgetting, why didn't he take notes? He had the parchment to do it—the stockpile Solomon had placed at our disposal was practically endless. His story was definitely sus. But he seemed so helpless, the little guy, that I somehow felt bad for him.

"Okay, come on in."

More than eagerly did he cross the threshold. And, once inside, he made himself at home, casting an inquiring eye all around.

"You are undoubtedly well taken care of here . . . Better than we are, much better. That's the advantage of enjoying certain favors from the king, isn't that right?"

A chuckle that attempted to establish complicity. But he would find no accomplice in me. He kept staring at me. Awkwardly, he decided to change the subject. He would now test the bonds of friendship. A real chatterbox: "Did you know I know your father?"

"Really?"

"Really." An air of triumph. "We were even friends... He probably doesn't remember me, but I always admired his energy... his leadership skills... Great man, your father. A bit handsy with the ladies, but a good guy." Realizing his gaffe, he backtracked: "Forgive me, I didn't mean to hurt your feelings. It's just that we were teenagers together, your father and I. Life drove us apart, but from time to time I caught wind of him: that he got married, that he had a gifted, intelligent daughter..."

Pretty, no. He had yet to resort to ass-kissing. He could label me as intelligent, as gifted, but he would omit all reference to physical appearance, which didn't stop short of amusing. But our conversation was starting me make me nervous, amusing or otherwise.

"Excuse me, small talk is okay and all, but, like I told you, I'm tired and tomorrow I have lots of work. If you could get straight to the point..."

"Straight to the point," as if he were talking to an invisible witness. "She wants me to get straight to the point... Fine, let's get straight to the point, then. What's a guy to do? Straight to the point. Here's the thing: As you know, the king directed us to evaluate your text and give feedback."

Hmm. This could be important. Solomon would surely take into account the opinion of the elders. It was therefore good that I was informed of the matter beforehand. But I didn't want to give away my vested interest to the little man. I asked, in the most casual way possible, what he thought. He smiled gleefully—Aha! I got you now, woman, I know your weak spot.

"We still haven't hammered out the details. And that's why I'm here. Like I said, I want to discuss a few issues in particular that seem—how do I put this?—rather intriguing."

Intriguing? What could be intriguing about such a clear and direct—if not poetic—text? He certainly noticed my frown, because he rushed to add: "Intriguing to me, of course. Intriguing, but..." again he flashed a smile, "fascinating. I've never read anything like it."

He paused and looked at me as if to study my reaction, then continued. "For such a young woman, you demonstrate great knowledge about life." He winked. "Is this knowledge from personal experience?"

Here we go; now we were in pervy territory, so to speak. Which, at that moment, didn't worry me: The little old man had a right to his fair share of vulgarity. Let him make two or three off-color jokes and leave—everything would be okay, especially since I didn't want to clash with the gnomes. So I responded with my own smile.

"It's simply my feminine instinct."

"Oh." He gave me side-eye, the dirty old goat. "Feminine instinct. Got it."

He stood there looking at me, unflinching, with debauchery written all over his face. Okay, yeah, the situation was way past cringe. This dumb conversation was busting my balls. What's more, my bladder was busting, I needed to pee, and this shrimp wasn't leaving. I decided to speed things up.

"But, anyhow, what was so different about what I wrote?"

He didn't immediately respond. He lowered his head and stared at the floor, his bald head shining in the torchlight. He finally looked up with a strange sparkle in his eyes. God, it was super creepy.

"Your text got me worked up. A lot. That part where you describe Adam and Eve making love on the dewy grass . . . Holy moly, that part is fire, baby! That part," he stopped himself, and with a brisk movement opened his robe.

The thing of nightmares: a rock-hard dick. An enormous penis, comically disproportionate to the diminutive stature of the man, an enormous dong that almost, I might add, threw him off-balance. I fought back the urge to crack up, guffaw, laugh my ass off at such a funny scene. But it wasn't the right time to laugh. It was time to put a wrench in what had already gone way too far.

"But what is this, old man?" I shrieked. "What is going through your head? Do you think that because you have the king's ear you can do whatever you please? I'm Solomon's wife, you nasty creep. If I told my husband, he would have you cut in two. What you're up to is an abomination! Abomination! I—"

He interrupted me, nervous and frantic. "Please," he whispered, almost crying. "Please! Yes, I know it's crazy, I could even pay for it with my life, but—do you know how long it's been since I had an erection? How long? Years. Decades. And it's not just old age; no, because in my family men hump into their hundreds. It went limp because of my wife, that viper. She never wanted anything to do with sex. She brutally rejected me whenever I tried anything. Go study your sacred texts, she would say. And I would go study. And study and study. What alternative did I have? I studied and studied. I knew everything about virtue and vice, about sin and abomination. Especially about abomination. Oh yes, when it came to abomination I knew it all. If you want I can make you a detailed list, with every abomination imaginable of every possible shape and size. Now, what good did studying do me? I was unhappy, my life bland. I dreamed of nothing but getting laid. I wished for a little bit of abomination. But no, abomination only came in books. In real life, only sadness and frustration. Then you appeared, and with a few lines you awoke in me a desire that I had taken for dead, finished... It's wonderful! It's a miracle!"

I didn't know what to say. On the one hand, his confession flattered me. If not as a woman, at least as a writer I had reached a significant milestone: I'd stimulated sudden and unexpected passion. The passion of a decrepit imp, true, but wasn't it precisely because he was a decrepit imp, semi-impotent, that my milestone was all the greater, especially considering my ugliness was a big capitis diminutio? The problem is that I wasn't in the mood. Losing my virginity to that sad shadow of a man—yes, that was an abomination. More importantly, however, I didn't want him, I wanted Solomon. Oh, if the king entered at that moment, he would see that, although ugly, I could give someone—even an old geezer, especially an old geezer—a boner. And perhaps that would deliver a shock to his system; perhaps, enraged, he would run the old man off, saying, No one lays a hand on my dear wife. Come here, babe, come, forget that gremlin, let us lie together and love each other. Vain hope, in the end. Solomon would not appear; maybe a guard would, if I screamed loud enough. But I didn't want to scream. I didn't want to hurt the man who, somehow, was paying me a compliment. So I told him that his declaration was touching, and that under different circumstances I wouldn't hesitate to receive him in my bed, but that at the moment there was no chance. All my attention was concentrated on my work, and only on my work.

He didn't listen. He slowly approached me, eyes bright, shaking with desire. And then, with surprising agility, he lunged at me. I repelled him, delicate but firmly. He tried again, and this time I pushed him away with such force that he fell on the floor and rolled. He tried to get up but got tangled in his robe and fell back to the floor. It was as comical as it was pathetic and, unable to hold it in any longer, I fell to the floor laughing. At which point he lost it. He stood, still reeling, and pointed an angry finger at me.

"Laugh at me, will you? At me, you desert bitch? Laughing because I wanted to screw you, something that no one will ever do, much less Solomon? You'll see, woman. You're disgusting, a monster, you're so ugly. Even so, I offered you sex out of pity. And you rejected it! You have nothing to lose, you fool!"

He looked at me, triumphant in his hate.

"Do you know who the elders charged with giving the final say on your text? Do you know who? Yours truly, that's who. I'm in charge of giving my recommendation on that crap you wrote. Guess what my recommendation will be now. Take a guess. This here is garbage, a disgrace! This here is an abomination!"

He tried to rip up the parchment—surely to throw the pieces in my face, but, its being quite literally tough as leather, he couldn't do it. He tried and tried—nothing. Finally, he threw it down on the floor and left, grumbling a string of obscenities.

I felt a sense of victory: Somehow my dignity was intact. Somehow vengeance against the mirror and all those who had mocked me was mine. Weird vengeance, sad vengeance, but vengeance.

There was another reason for my satisfaction. My text had just been tested, however creepily so. The old man was a sort of guinea pig. If I had managed to drive him crazy, Solomon would find me irresistible. What I had to do was this: stick with lewd descriptions until I lured him into my room screaming, I can't take it anymore! I want you now, I want you all to myself! And I would say to him, The text is all yours, but so too is its author. And we would live happily ever after. Of that much I was certain, and so, pleased with myself, I went to sleep.

The incident with the old man, however, would have serious consequences, as I soon found out. I woke up early the next morning to a guard knocking at my door—and this time they were strong, insistent knocks. Solomon ordered me to appear in his throne room. I went, with a bad feeling in the pit of my stomach.

There was the king, seated on his throne. At his side, the six microbes, each of them frowning: The old man probably hadn't said nice things about me. I prepared myself for a chewing out, but what came next was worse.

As always, Solomon chose his words carefully and said that he had already formed an opinion about what I had written. My stylistic qualities were appreciated, but the same couldn't be said for the narrative itself, which included some distortions. Considering the importance of the book that was being prepared, guidelines would have to be adopted to avoid what he called, euphemistically, accidental detours. From then on I was to stay in my writing lane. The content would be provided by the elders, who also had the power to veto anything I wrote. As he spoke, I looked at the dirty old geezer. He tried to exude an air of neutrality and distance, but he was clearly delighted with the king's words.

I was defeated, soundly defeated. My hopes of sexting Solomon via parchment were sunk. Worse: Now the old men were in charge, and I didn't have anyone to defend me. Like the king said, with their decades-long repute for erudition (all of them had served David, Solomon's father), and thanks to their powerful connections, the elders were a pretty big deal. Even though they didn't occupy government positions, they did form a sort of informal supreme council, which conferred on the royal house a portion of its legitimacy. I didn't have the slightest chance against them. I therefore accepted the verdict in silence. The only card I had left to play was submission.

The next day I found myself writing our history exactly how they wanted it. The woman being manufactured from Adam's rib. The woman paying heed to the snake. The woman eating of the fruit of the Tree of the Knowledge of Good and Evil. In short, the woman fucking everything up. And then came the story of Cain and Abel. (Two sons: no daughters. In other words, they wouldn't have the chance to reproduce, not even by incest.) Abel, the shepherd (of sheep, not goats), and Cain, the farmer, quarrel instead of choosing to join forces in an agropastoral venture, which would be more logical and profitable. God rejects Cain's offering, for reasons only he and the elders understand. Jealousy and foul play. A blood feud ensues, to the delight of the dirty old geezer. The text would now unleash his wrath, his pent-up rancor.

My tribulations didn't stop there. On the same day that I wrote the story about said crime, a palace servant informed me of what had happened to the shepherd boy. I imagined he had left in peace after having handed over the parchment to the soldiers. But no, not only did he refuse to hand over my message, willing to defend it with his life, but he tried to fight off the soldiers. He ended up losing his arm, hewn off by the swing of a sword. And then, he vanished.

As one can easily imagine, his story left me shaken to the core. Poor guy, he'd paid dearly for his willingness to help me. Worse: At the heart of it all was a completely pointless sacrifice that left me upset and depressed. I would no longer ask my father to kidnap the king to force him to make love to me. Truth be told, I'd given up on that idea. Sex was now relegated to plan C or D.

I returned to work, which became extremely difficult. With their reinforced authority, the elders rubbed it in. They forced me to redo what I wrote several times. And what I wrote, like the episode of Cain and Abel, only made me dry heave.

I tried to fight back. I wanted them to at least recognize the inconsistencies in their gloomy history of that first murder. According to the elders, after being duly cursed, Cain protested to the Lord: "I shall be a fugitive and a vagabond on the earth. All who find me may kill me." But who could his potential killer be if, up to that point in the narrative, excluding slain Abel, only Adam, Eve, and Cain existed? I asked the elders about it, in a respectful tone, as they insisted, but deep down I enjoyed the possible perplexity the issue would cause.

But they were never perplexed. They looked at each other, sure, but as if to say, She's as dumb as she is ugly, and one of them dryly responded: "Write and don't ask questions."

The narrative continued with one catastrophe after another. Explanation: According to the elders, evil and abomination—by the looks of it, they thought little of anything else—were the norm among Adam's descendants who, periodically, needed to be punished. Like Adam and Eve, like Cain, except their punishments were restrictive, personalized. The elders' script prescribed a wide range of comprehensive, spectacular punishments, real overkill as far as being the scourge of humanity. In the next chapter, they announced that it would rain for forty days and forty nights. That, to me, coming from a desert, was beyond belief. And to think that God had never listened to our pleas for rain: All we got for our prayers were miserable little sprinkles. But the elders weren't thinking in terms of agricultural benefits. Their downpour would flood the face of the Earth. All creatures would be exterminated, they gleefully announced.

The whole thing really left me down in the dumps. I went to my room and cried and cried for hours on end. I'd lost all hope of seducing Solomon, lost the will to work on the text. I'd lost everything; all I had left was my bereft and eternal ugliness. My life had no meaning.

I decided to end it once and for all. In death I would search out the solution to my torment. First, I would write a letter to Solomon explaining my decision and professing that I would love him forever. Next, I would slit my throat with a knife and spill my blood all over the parchment, possibly making it illegible, but that was of little consequence to me.

My messiness saved me from death. My room had a small kitchen, and cutlery, but I couldn't find the damn knife. I remembered that I had used it the night before to peel an apple, but where had I put it? It had disappeared, as if by magic. I began to look for it haphazardly.

Right then, someone knocked on my door: another one of the king's guards. Solomon wanted to see me. I wanted to tell the guy, Not right now, I'm about to kill myself, inform your king that the ugly one is leaving this world behind. But then I wondered if destiny had come knocking or, what for me was more important, proof of the monarch's wisdom and sensibility. Surely, he'd realized what was going on (the poor little thing is capable of doing something stupid, she left here so desperate) and he had sent for me. Even so, I hesitated. Would it be worth it to answer his call? What could Solomon say to me that I didn't already know. But I had nothing to lose. Like the elders of my village used to say, There's always time to kill yourself.

I got dressed and followed the guard. I found the king alone, not on his throne, but on a comfortable divan. Apparently, he'd already shrugged off the most recent events; he was in a good mood, smiling. He stood, came to my side, took me by the hand, and gestured for me to sit with him. Despite everything, he stated, he was very happy with my work—which greatly surpassed his expectations. He hugged me, caressed my face. And when I began to cry, he said: "Let it out, dear wife, shed your tears; it will make you feel better."

And it did make me feel better. I left there certain that if he didn't love me, he was fond of me, a fondness that could, in time, turn to love. I needed to be patient, and very persistent. Like the farmers back home when they tried to cultivate their fragile plants in the parched earth. One day the flower of love would blossom there.

I went to the elders' study with a new outlook. Encouraged I was not; comforted, yes. And luckily the narrative I had to transcribe wasn't all that bad. Yes, a deluge was annihilating humanity and all living things (like, what had brussels sprouts ever done to anyone?)—except, obviously, sparing the fishes who took to that immense body of water like, well, like fish to water. But God does cut humanity some slack and lets Noah off the hook in the Ark. I had fun imagining the animals boarding that Ark, daily life there inside . . . At least it was something interesting.

It was more than that. It was revealing. Suddenly I saw myself in Noah's place, on the bow of an enormous and strange ship, contemplating the immensity of the waters, that vast ocean without islands, without beaches, the liquid surface reflecting the unfathomable face of God. Like Noah, I was a survivor, a survivor of misfortune. I would not drown in the ocean of my tears; my writing would be my little, modest Ark. Rejected by a text in which I no longer recognized myself, I would take refuge not in the lines, but in between the lines. There, I would leave a silent and cryptic message, a message that, like a bottle tossed in the sea, would possibly reach someone in a near or distant future. And I would be there, celebrating the love of Adam and Eve, and of the many men and women whose names didn't appear in the collected works of old men, but who weren't any less important as human beings because of that. Anonymous I, too, would remain, but the warmth of my flame would be felt in the manuscript one way or another.

That night I looked in a mirror. Once again, I thought I detected change: My features were now a little less harsh, the expression in my eyes a little softer. I was certain that I was on the right track—in life and on the page. Regarding the narrative that was to be written, many generations would come and go before I reached my destination, but I would do it, of that much I was sure.

And the generations came and went in the elders' account, which now abandoned humanity as a whole and focused on the Hebrews, starting with the patriarchs. This was their home turf. When it came to patriarchy, they certainly knew their stuff, and they made it very clear that it was a perfect model, the daddy of all models. It occurred to me that perhaps this was a political move: Patriarchs in the beginning, judges later, kings at the end; they were suggesting that there was a continuum of power that went back to time immemorial and culminated with their patron, Solomon. Their approach I could not, and did not, question. One could only oppose their gross Machiavellianism with another, kinder Machiavellianism, a Machiavellianism of camouflaged sentiment. I retreated so that later, like a gazelle, I could bound over their obstacles and frolic through the prairie of love.

So I stuck to writing the history of said patriarchs, figures who seemed rather baffling to me, on display in their anxiousness to please the Lord. Jehovah commands, Abraham obeys, even when his obedience entails sacrificing his own son. At most he dares to bargain, thanks to which he gets the Lord to progressively reduce the necessary quorum of righteous people to save Sodom.

In the name of justice, women did make an appearance also, and they had some importance and dignity. Of course, they weren't immune to human weakness. Sarah screwed over Hagar, with whom Abraham had a son, but that was all part of the tribal power struggle. Much worse shenanigans were had when that old creep made a pass at me. And he, by the way, demanded his pound of flesh for the supposed offense that I had inflicted upon him. He didn't miss a chance to humiliate me.

"Write down: Rebecca, Isaac's wife, was very beautiful. Did you hear me? She was very beautiful. Isaac would never pick an ugly woman. Jacob either. He fell in love with Rachel because she was beautiful. Ugliness has no place in sacred texts. Ugliness is an abomination."

Offenses aside, writing about the patriarchs had an unexpected effect on me: It helped me understand my father. He obviously considered himself a descendant of Abraham, Isaac, and Jacob. In that light, his arrogance seemed understandable to me. The image I had of my father changed: I remembered him with nostalgia, with tenderness even. Distance minimized his defects; with time I would forgive him. But then he turned up at the palace.

In a surprise twist, he arrived without notice. And he didn't come on account of me. The stated objective of his trip was to visit the Temple, which he was periodically supposed to do to fulfill his religious duties; in reality, however, he'd come to reinforce his political ties with Solomon, and obviously he would take the opportunity to see me. After all, I was his daughter and, to boot, married to the king.

It was Solomon himself who brought him to my room. He opened the door and announced, smiling: "I have a surprise for you. A visitor."

My father burst into my room, as loud and obnoxious as ever. "Look at my daughter! The girl I held in my arms—now she's a queen!" He hugged me enthusiastically, then he looked me up and down: "Yes ma'am, you're really living it up here, very fancy." He didn't say I looked pretty, obviously—that would be asking too much of him.

Solomon observed the scene with an amused smile; then, after saying he had lots to do, he excused himself and left.

"A real mensch, your king," commented my father. He looked around, satisfied with what he was seeing. "You've settled in nicely here. This room of yours is bigger than our whole house."

He asked what my life was like at the palace, what I did all day. I answered evasively. Suddenly, he noticed the shelves full of scrolls. He frowned. "So this writing thing wasn't just a phase? I thought you had outgrown that bullshit!"

I was fed up with the act: "Yes, I'm writing, and it's the only thing I do all day long." I added, "It's a job for the king."

He, clearly offended, "A job?" Work was something for slaves, not a royal wife. "What's this about? My daughter working for the king, playing the role of an employee? I didn't give you to Solomon for this. I gave you to him so that you would have an honorable place in the harem. Instead, you're here, writing! You've got to be kidding!"

Furious, he went silent. But then he immediately went back on the attack, this time in search of a scapegoat. A sacrificial goat.

"It's your fault. Who told you to learn to read and write? I knew this whole thing was a dead end. I told your mom: A woman has no business writing, a woman's business is doing something else in bed. I don't even know how to read and write, and I'm the boss. Why did you have to ruffle feathers? You're ugly enough as it is, why'd you go and get book learning? There you have it: The other seven hundred women are in the harem, having a good time, eating the best of the best, bathing, wearing perfume, and here you are, your ass wasting away in a chair, working on those goddamn scrolls. Do you realize how embarrassing this is for me? What am I gonna say when I go to the Temple and run into other tribal bigwigs, huh? What am I gonna say? That my daughter works more than a slave? I can't understand what's going on here. Frankly, I don't get it."

No sooner had he spoken than something occurred to him, his face immediately clouding over. "I want to know one thing," he said, in an ominous tone. "Has he deflowered you yet?"

Well, shit, I didn't have the guts to tell him. I was suddenly that scared little girl he yelled at and hit every now and again: because I had spilled my cup of goat's milk, because I hadn't swept the house—I was always doing something wrong, on top of having been born ugly, which was also my fault and a monstrous shortcoming. He would never forgive me if I told him the truth. It would be the end of the world. Maybe I also felt bad for the man. He was, after all, little more than an ignorant villager whose greatest achievement would be to see his daughter as the king's favorite wife. So I decided to lie.

"Yes, father. He already deflowered me. He fulfilled his obligation."

"Thank goodness," he said, still angry, but now a bit more relieved. Something had been salvaged from the disaster: The marriage had been consummated, his honor was intact. Happy to change the subject, he began to talk about the Temple, about marble and cedarwood, everything coated in gold—luxury at its finest. Sacrificing at the Temple was a real treat. In his enthusiasm, he had sent three sheep to be killed, even though only one would have been sufficient to settle his debts with the higher-ups. He considered himself a just man, even though his enemies, who weren't few in number, thought otherwise, and went around spreading—

He stopped talking. He stood there in silence, on his face—and it was a tortured face—a gloomy expression. And then, in a contained but suspicious tone, he asked: "Are you gonna talk about me?"

"What?" I didn't know what he was referring to.

"In that book. You gonna talk about me?"

The question sounded so absurd that I began to laugh. I laughed and laughed while he, confused and irritated, looked at me without a clue. I finally managed to settle down.

"No," I said, wiping my eyes. "I'm not going to write about you."

"Oh, good. I don't want anyone writing about me. When I tell the story of my life, it'll get told my way. And whoever writes it will be a trustworthy scribe. As for you, you can talk about kings and prophets and whatever, but not about me, no. That's the last thing I need."

His arrogance, however, did a bad job of covering up his disappointment. Even if for a brief moment, deep down he nurtured the hope of ending up in the narrative alongside Solomon, the powerful king, builder of the Temple—even if it were only for having given his daughter in marriage to the sovereign.

He was so disconcerted that I decided to change the subject. I asked about my mother and my sisters. He made a vague gesture, as if to say: No news with them, nothing to tell on the home front. And then I had an idea: Maybe he knew about the shepherd boy. I worked up the nerve to ask about him.

"The goatfucker?" He laughed scornfully. "He got what was coming to him. After he left the village he came here to Jerusalem, certainly plotting some grift or another. But something went wrong and he got in a fight with Solomon's soldiers. Those fellas cut off his arm. He only escaped death because someone cauterized the stump with boiling oil. That's when he went back to the village."

He frowned. "In fact, he told the oddest story. Said the soldiers attacked him because he refused to hand over a letter—a letter you had written to me. Did you write me a letter?"

"Letter?" I would never have thought myself capable of such hypocrisy. I convincingly acted surprised. I was getting good at lying, no doubt. "No. I didn't write any letter."

"I knew it," he said, triumphant. "I knew that rat bastard was lying. A very second-rate guy, never pulled his own weight. I was even good to him. I should've stoned him to death. But no, I felt sorry for him—and that's how it went down."

"And what happened to the dude?" I asked, in the same casual tone as before.

"I sent him away. Off to schmooze some other chump."

"And did he leave?"

"He did. And do you know what he's up to now? He joined a band of religious fanatics led by some crazy old man. They claim to be defenders of the faith, but I don't think they're much more than bandits. They go around attacking Solomon's soldiers. Utter madness. Shameless tomfoolery. Challenging the king's authority, who ever heard of such a thing? We've never had a monarch like Solomon, never will again. Just take a look at the Temple. Just look at the palace. And the reputation he upholds—Israel never had a king with such a good reputation abroad. His renown is well deserved, of course. Such an intelligent man, so wise . . ."

He began to tell the story about the two women who had a dispute over a newborn, but I was no longer listening to him. I was thinking about how the shepherd boy had sacrificed himself on my behalf. It was my obligation to do something for the poor guy. But how could I help him, a fugitive, without knowing his whereabouts? It was too late now. I would have to live with my guilt.

My father stated that he was going to the throne room, where Solomon would receive him. I asked if he wanted me to go with. No, he didn't want me to. His business with the king was no business of mine. His hearing with the king would probably last an hour, and afterward my father would hit the road: It was a long journey back to the village. So we said our goodbyes then and there. He told me to take care, to think long and hard about what I was going to write in that book. On impulse, he hugged me, and then, looking at me with tears in his eyes, he confided that his big dream was to have male grandchildren who would continue his lineage, preferably adding royal blood to it—which only I could do. He asked when I would have a son. I said I didn't know, that I couldn't foretell the future. That's the king's domain, only he decides.

"I'm going to drop him a hint," he said with a smile that made a go at camaraderie but fell flat and was awkward. He hugged me and left.

The next day I was at it again, writing.

We quickly fell into a routine. Every day, the elders would brief me. Consulting mountains of scrolls and debating among themselves, they would decide what was important for the book. The dirty old geezer—at that point putting on airs of deep concentration—would act as narrator. It was also up to him to impose the restrictions on my work, restrictions that diminished as I got the hang of things. My north star was never to make anything up. Diving into the text, I was to set aside all personal vision, all my biases. I was to be neutral, impersonal. No side notes. Such commentary, the elders told me, would be left to wise men in future generations. And I obeyed. Of course, I still wondered about certain passages. Why didn't Joseph bone Potiphar's wife, making everyone happy, including Potiphar himself? I kept that doubt to myself. The old men would be offended if I asked. At any rate, I didn't want to start a shouting match; I'd lost my appetite for such things. In my moments of greatest depression, I thought about running away, about fleeing to the harem, about going anywhere where I wouldn't have to write or think or debate. But then Solomon's face would come to mind, and my love for him would take a powerful hold on me. I would sort of get my energy back and return to work, regardless of how boring it was. Little did I know my fate still had a difficult ordeal in store for me.

It happened one night. After I had gotten into my work routine, my sleep schedule, already irregular, went off the rails, a train wreck of dreamless sleep. No lean-fleshed cows or fat-fleshed cows; Joseph would waste his time with me. But that night it was different. At one point I woke up with a start, hearing giggles, whispers, gasps of pleasure—what was going on? Was I losing my mind?

No, I wasn't. The noises came from the room next door. One of Solomon's bedrooms—he had several scattered throughout the palace. It was also said that he sometimes went from bedroom to bedroom, tending to the women there, which smelled like propaganda for his sexual prowess; more probable was that it was a question of security. But, anyway: There was the king—I immediately identified his voice, his characteristic laugh—receiving a woman from the harem. Evidently, he was having a good time. From what I could hear, it was a no-holds-barred contest: now suck it, now doggy-style.

That he was getting some wasn't the problem, he had the right. That he was flipping through the entire catalog of abominations from beginning to end: A-OK. But why in that room? Could it be that he was unaware that I was on the other side of the wall, sitting in my bed, wide-eyed, fists clenched, all ears, hearing it all?

Yes, he knew. He knew everything. Wasn't he the wisest man in the world, the man who spoke to birds? He knew, of course he did. And I knew it was one of two scenarios: Either he didn't care about my presence, or he did care about my presence.

If he didn't care about my presence, I needed to give up on my fantasies once and for all: Oh you, yes you, abandon all hope. That's right, you, the ugly one who only knows how to write, throw in the towel, take a hike, forget about the Solomon in your dreams, the guy who woke you up in the middle of the night signaling, with his orgasmic moans, the insignificance of your suffering in love.

A cruel conclusion. But at least I was facing reality head-on. I would have to decide if I wanted to keep up the act or not. It did me no good to keep pretending I was the king's wife. Either I accepted my role of writing the book, without further expectations, or I would leave for good, preferably to some distant place: the desert, for example. There I would live in a cave, alone with my pain and sorrow. And my stone.

But there was another possibility: like, maybe he did remember that I was in the room beside him. And if he remembered, why was he making obscene noises? Sadism? That wasn't his style. Was he flaunting his potency? But why? To win me over? Me, who'd given myself to him fruitlessly?

There was only one possible answer: Solomon wasn't thinking about sex, he was thinking about the book. He wasn't hurting for sex. In his case, supply clearly exceeded demand. He had more women than he knew what to do with, even when taking into account his legendary magical powers. For him, screwing was probably a sacrifice, a job requirement. Not the book. The book would satisfy his need for recognition and affirmation. The book, as he himself had said, would consecrate him. Now, the book was me. That became more evident with each passing day. But it also became evident, and he was too smart not to notice, that my patience for the work was not limitless. So he led me on with oblique promises, made in indirect ways. A voice-over, so to speak: Get it written promptly and my bed is yours—come on down, all the pleasure that these moans, sighs, and giggles represent can be yours. Just sign here to open your pleasure account. One day, you'll be able to withdraw everything that is rightfully yours, with interest. And then you will see that Solomon is capable. Ugly or not, you will live orgasmic nights of ecstasy.

The fact of the matter was that their soundtrack awoke my desire. I was so horny (and I missed my stone. At least it had never humiliated me, never let me down)! Anyway, I had to recognize that if it was a matter of trickery, the king—capable of talking to birds—had been very successful. I had fallen into his trap.

In a way, I had become a slave to his ploy. Like the Hebrews in Egypt, burdened with building the pyramids, every day I stacked my stones on his literary monument. In the hope that I would be treated kindly, I submitted to a merciful pharaoh. But it was servitude nonetheless, and from my servitude no Moses would set me free; the waters of the sea (and in Jerusalem we were far from the sea) wouldn't part so that I could head to the Promised Land. Unless the shepherd boy, my poor shepherd boy, came with his guerrillas to free me. Very unlikely. It would be, in the end, a failed attempt: Solomon's soldiers would finish him off in the blink of an eye.

I got used to the orgies in the bedroom next door. I got used to my work routine. There was nothing else I could do. I couldn't leave the palace; at most I was permitted to visit the harem from time to time. The women now looked at me differently, with admiration and even with a certain reverence. I continued to be the ugly one, but a respected ugly one, the ugly one to whom Solomon had entrusted an important task. For my part, I had also changed in relation to them. The contempt I had felt for this group of women, after the failure of the protest movement I had tried to organize, now gave way to a resigned tolerance, understanding, and even warmth. Like me, they had come from faraway places; like me, they were there primarily to strengthen alliances; like me, they dreamed of the king's bed—and, like me, many loved him. Unlike me, they were mostly beautiful women. Also unlike me, they didn't know how to read or write. They had nothing to do with their lives other than wait for the king to send for them. Yet, at the end of the day, they were all women, and a question I asked myself when I would see them at the harem or the patio, talking or playing around or singing: Could I possibly have a friend there, someone who could play the role in my life that my sisters had tried in vain to take on, all while being so fiercely repulsed by me?

In the moments when such doubts assailed me, the story would coincidently suffer an inflection, an unexpected change that would surprise even me. We had already left Moses behind, the plagues of Egypt, the crossing of the Red Sea, the long journey through Sinai; Joshua had already toppled the walls of Jericho; Canaan had been conquered after vicious battles... In other words, more of the same: lots of fighting, lots of bloodshed.

Then, suddenly, Ruth and Naomi appeared. It came as a real shock, something with magical powers that pulled me out of my habitual apathy and mobilized my emotions all over again. The story of friendship between those two women, mother-in-law and daughter-in-law, Jew and Moabite, old and young, moved me to tears. I spent hours thinking about them, about their sworn loyalties. And so I sat and worked, pouring my heart and soul into it. I wrote three versions before coming to the conclusion that the text couldn't be improved upon. When I finally read my work to the elders, I even began to sob. Normally, they would have reacted with irritation—Just what we need, throw in a woman to write a sacred text, women can't be objective, they can't even control their emotions—but this time they were respectfully silent and, I would say, supportive. They knew that my emotions were born from a profound identification with the two women.

In the days that followed, I thought a lot about the story of Ruth and Naomi. It was as if I had written a message, not to Solomon, like I had in the case of Adam and Eve, but to myself. It abruptly occurred to me that I didn't need to go it alone; yes, my royal husband ignored me, my family was far away (and even if they were nearby, it would make no difference), but I could seek out solace in a friend. That word sounded refreshing to me; in the village, for example, I had never made friends with anyone. I was the marginalized, ugly one. A situation that had been repeated at the harem, but something told me that someone who understood me ought to exist among all those women, someone who would be my BFF. I had to find a friend.

And I found her. It was on a sultry summer night. I had tried working on the manuscript for several hours, but I was unproductive. After the story of Ruth and Naomi, the narrative was no longer of interest to me. It felt deprived of emotion. Exhausted, I set the parchment aside and went to lie down. But I was unable to fall asleep either, so I decided to go out to get a bit of air. I walked aimlessly down the palace corridors, the guards observing me with curiosity and distrust. At last, I reached the harem garden.

A large moon illuminated the place, which at that hour—nearly midnight—was deserted. But there was one woman sitting there. I only knew her face; I knew she was a concubine, not a wife. She smiled when she saw me.

"I see you can't sleep," she paused, then added, "like me. Sleep abandoned me years ago. So I come here to think about life a little, to reminisce about the past."

"Does it help?" I asked.

She smiled again. "I don't know. But, in the absence of something better... Come, sit here."

I sat and we began to talk. First about banal things, later about serious things—we talked and talked. It was as if we had always been friends.

Her name was Mikol. Although still pretty and sensual, she was no longer altogether young; truth be told, she was one of the first concubines Solomon had acquired, at a time when the market for women was saturated.

"The king bought me on the cheap. I was already a concubine; my first lord was a brutal man. He hit me every night. When he announced that I would be going to the royal palace, that he had sold me to Solomon, I was afraid. Was I not trading one tyrant for a worse one? But when I saw our king, our man, I immediately fell in love. Like you. And, I should say, it was requited love. He was much younger then, fiercer, but also more inexperienced. A sad man. Wise, but sad—wisdom doesn't make anyone happy. On top of that, his daddy issues had left him deeply wounded. Because he was a real stud, King David. His son knew that and it hurt him to know it. The poor guy was useless in bed. One day he confessed to me: that's why he'd bought a concubine, because he didn't know how to make love. He asked me to initiate him in sex, something he couldn't expect from his wives who were as inexperienced as he was. I accepted the mission with great pleasure. I soon saw that I would have to take it slowly, guiding him step by step. Which wasn't easy, given his anxiety, his fear of failure. Sometimes we would be in bed, him on top of me, and out of nowhere he would say: I can't, I just can't. I would soothe him, get him in the mood again, and then the volcano would erupt."

She went quiet, her eyes lost for a moment, remembering the good old days.

"Those were weeks of passion," she continued. "Afterward, he acquired other concubines. And his wives kept arriving by the dozen. In other words, Solomon had his hands full..."

She laughed. "Hands, among other things. I wound up on the back burner, you know? But it didn't matter, I knew it would happen one day. I became a sort of consultant for sexual advice. He would send for me: Listen, Mikol, that wife who came from the North is standoffish, what do I do? And then I would teach him how to proceed. Mikol, the olive-skinned one is really jealous, how do I fix it? I would give him suggestions. When the number of women grew, he would again consult my opinion on how to organize in a way that would meet all their needs. He first came up with the idea to invite to bed the woman whose birthday it was that day. I mentioned to him that many women could have birthdays on the same date, which would complicate things. Use your own criteria, I suggested, and don't share them with anyone. Love requires mystery. Impressed, he said I was wise, wiser than he. And he didn't forget me as a woman either. Whenever he felt like a wild romp in the sack, he would send for me."

"And what was he like in bed?" I wondered why I asked her that question. If anyone else spoke to me about their lovemaking with Solomon I would have died of jealousy and envy. But with Mikol, I immediately felt I could talk about the subject that was, for me, so painful. Was that friendship? Yes, it was a budding friendship, I confirmed, delighted. I don't know if she felt the same. But she responded openly:

"Well. It wasn't out of this world, but it was good. With my training, modesty aside, he got much better. On a scale of one to ten, I would give him a seven. Or even eight, depending on the day. He had his moments of inspiration, others when he couldn't concentrate. For a burdened king with a troubled mind, he wasn't all that bad. What he lacked in execution he made up for in kindness. After the fact, it was nice to talk to him. Great mind. He liked to talk to birds ... Great mind. He knew every position in bed under the sun. You had to be there. He learned from some kings from the East."

Perhaps not wanting to hurt my feelings—but it was an unnecessary precaution—Mikol made it clear that everything she was telling me was in the past. She was a turned page in Solomon's love story.

"I was important, now I'm not. But it's okay, remembering is enough. Especially since there was another after him."

Another? What? How had she been managed to have contact with another man?

She winked. "I live in the harem, dear. I'm not a prisoner there. Of course, it's not easy to sneak out, but there is always a way. And there are a lot of good-looking men out there. Not long ago, I met a young fellow who was fantastic in bed. A gigolo on the side, but—"

She stopped herself, sat there in silence with a lost look. She sighed. "My love affairs are of no interest. Let's talk about you, that's more important."

She wanted to know where I came from, what my life had been like, what my relationship with Solomon was like. I told her about my fiasco with the king. To my surprise, she found it funny, said that I shouldn't worry: Sooner or later my time would come. And, to my surprise, she was really interested in the book I was preparing. Interested, no. Amazed.

"Writing a book like that, my friend, is the crème de la crème. I'd love to make an appearance in it. At Solomon's side, for example. But there are so many people. Seven hundred wives, three hundred concubines . . . Impossible. There is no place for me. Unless in an ellipsis . . ."

She didn't know how to read or write, but she knew her punctuation marks: the period, the comma—which always left her pensive—the question and exclamation marks, which provoked belly laughs. And the dash—she also knew the dash. All in all, she really liked the ellipsis. She knew it was meant to make a forlorn person think about life, about the world . . .

"Yes, maybe there is a place for me in the ellipsis . . . The person who comes across those three little dots will say, Hmm, but then Solomon's story isn't merely what's described in words . . . There's more to it. And upon wondering what else there might be, perhaps from the long list of possibilities a certain concubine will come to mind . . . She was a good lay . . . A great lay . . ."

I promised her that I would add ellipses to the story about Solomon. To be honest, it was unlikely that I would get the chance to do so. As much as she adored punctuation marks, the elders detested them; what good were question marks or exclamation marks if God neither questions nor marvels? Why ellipses if God never elides?

That was the only time I lied to Mikol. In the few months that we spent together—and we would meet up in the garden almost every night—our relationship was defined by weakness. Weakness and affection. I loved her. Mikol was everything to me: the mother I never had, the father who wasn't a jerk, the sister who didn't lie, the husband who didn't reject me. Around her, I felt happy. Not completely happy. Because of Solomon, of course. She tried to console me. He's going to send for you, she would say, it's only a matter of time. How long, I wanted to know: a long time, a short time? Weeks, days, years? One day, when I impatiently demanded an answer, she let it slip, something she'd never done until then. I think she was getting it off her chest.

"You have time," she said. "I'm the one who does not."

I didn't understand. Why didn't she have time? She wasn't a young woman, but she was far from being old. Why didn't she have time?

In response, she grabbed my hand and put it over her belly. There was something in her stomach, some mass, hard as a rock. A pregnancy was the first thought that crossed my mind, and I was immediately overtaken by jealousy, as violent as it was absurd. Despite what she had told me—that she no longer had sexual relations—I thought she was expecting a child, Solomon's child. She would have to take care of the baby—of Solomon's baby—and not me.

It took no effort for her to guess what I was thinking. And she smiled, with sadness. "No, I'm not pregnant. That would be tough at my age, right? And then . . . I can't bring a child into the world, I'm not worthy of it. No, it's not a pregnancy. I have a tumor in there, a tumor that ceaselessly grows. It means I'm very sick. That I'm going to die soon."

I couldn't believe what she was telling me, mostly because of her resigned serenity. She had a tumor? And she was going to die? But why? Why did she accept such an unjust, monstrous fate? I was suddenly filled with enormous guilt. There I was, complaining about my ugliness, as if it were the greatest tragedy in the universe, and poor Mikol was dying. Selfish me, not even paying attention to the severity of her condition. Now I noticed how gaunt and sunken she had become over the last few weeks. She was pale, weak. I thought she'd been dieting—she was susceptible to fad diets, there was one time when she would only eat oranges or pomegranates. But I was wrong, it had nothing to do with her diet. It was an illness, a serious and deadly illness.

"But we have to do something," I said, barely holding back my tears. "I'm going to talk to the palace doctor, he's a good doctor, he—"

Gently, she cut me off: "The palace doctor says it's a lost cause."

I couldn't take it anymore: I burst out in tears. I cried for her, for me. I'd found a friend, someone I could confide in—and that friend was going to leave me now. I want to die, I would tell her, I want to die with you, because wherever you go, I will go, and where you die, there will I be buried also. With a smile (which, by the way, had an element of wistful skepticism—my wailing and gnashing of teeth surely seemed somewhat over the top to her), she would attempt to console me: I will never abandon you, I will always be with you in spirit—the types of things a charitable, dying person says to a child, to a friend.

Her illness progressed rapidly. In a matter of days she was skin and bones. The tumor grew shockingly fast, and Mikol became so frail that she was unable to get out of bed. Sitting by her side I looked on in horror at her devastated body, reduced to an appendage of the sinister mass, now easily visible, obscenely visible. Her breasts showed through her half-open nightgown, which just weeks before I had still admired, beautiful as they were. Those breasts—what had happened to them? One of them, the left one or the right one, I don't remember anymore, was still a bit perky, as if fearfully holding on for dear life; but the other, the right or the left one, was saggy, depressed, weary: That breast had already given up the fight, that breast was walking through the Valley of the Shadow of Death, swaying to and fro. Hello, Shadow of Death, here I am, what're you gonna do about it, huh, Shadow of Death? I would rather have skipped this leg of the journey, or at least stayed behind like my sister breast, but what am I supposed to do, Shadow of Death? I was always hasty, always preferred to get straight to it; when Solomon used to suck on us, I was always the first to tense up and have my nipple go hard, and now here I am, a dried raisin, worse than a dried raisin, because a dried raisin is sweet and nutritious and I'm not even that. I'm just a memory, a bitter memory. That's what she told me, her breast, either the right or the left one.

That's what her wrecked body told me. Because of the putrid smell that it gave off, they took her out to the concubine pavilion and placed her in an isolated stall, where I would visit her every day. It came at the cost of frequent fights with the elders. They claimed I was falling behind, demanded I work more and more. I didn't have the will to write, but Mikol urged me to keep at it, so I would sit down at the table and work and work. The narrative was now approaching our era: We had made it to the Book of Samuel. Saul had just been declared king, and the royal house would reach its culmination with Solomon. But I had little interest in his story of struggles and intrigues. I only thought of Mikol, of Mikol dying in her stall. I would often turn in the parchment with ink smeared by my tears.

One night, one of the elders came to talk to me; he wanted to know what was going on. I still didn't care for those old geezers, and normally I would have responded rudely: It's none of your business; you mind yours and I'll mind mine. But for some reason I decided to tell him what was happening: My friend was dying and I couldn't take care of her. I had to write a narrative that meant nothing to me. It was merely a testament to the king's vanity.

He wasn't happy: "Don't say such things," he said, "that history is important; it's the history of a people who follow the divine plan."

That was even more revolting to me. "Divine plan? What piece-of-shit plan lets a poor woman die who never did anything bad to anyone? That God of yours only wants sacrifices, nothing more. Fixing something would be nice for a change, but he never fixes anything. Look at what happened to poor Job. He covered the man in boils all because of a wager with the devil. Divine plan! I'll show you divine plan!"

He could have gotten mad at me, the elder. He could have yelled "Abomination! Abomination!" or something like that. He could have ratted me out to Solomon. But he didn't. Why? Was it because he took pity on my suffering? Or was it because he needed me? I don't know. I only know that he chose to console me. He said that actually Mikol was suffering divine punishment; everyone knew she was a transgressor; she had cheated on Solomon with numerous men: courtiers, palace guards, and even with a partially maimed shepherd boy who at one time wandered around the palace walls, playing his flute. Solomon had forgiven her—but he couldn't save her from divine wrath.

His revelation left me floored. Yes, I knew that Mikol had had her affairs. But the shepherd boy? Was that why he had snooped around the palace? Regardless, she hadn't done anything wrong. If Solomon could have a thousand women, why couldn't Mikol have an affair here and there? Whatever the case, his explanation shut me up. I told the elder that I would go back to work, and that's what I did; I went back to work. I stayed up until dawn, writing nonstop.

The next morning I found that Mikol had taken a turn. The harem overseer, who was there, shook her head. It was a question of days, of hours, maybe. Mikol asked her to leave; she wanted to talk to me alone. The woman left, and I leaned over Mikol's bed.

"I have a favor to ask," she said, almost in a whisper. "My last request."

She wanted to see Solomon before dying. She wanted to make love to him for the last time; then, and only then, would she rest in peace. She held my hand in her feeble, dry little claws. "Please, help me. If you ask, he'll listen. He doesn't need me anymore, but he has great need of you."

What could I do? It had been a while since I'd even seen him. I didn't know if he would receive me. But I would do anything for Mikol.

I left and went looking for the courtier in charge of granting an audience. "I need to talk to the king. It's urgent."

He looked at me suspiciously—no love lost there—and consulted his scroll with the royal schedule. "It won't do. He's all booked today and tomorrow. Numerous foreign delegations . . . It just won't do."

I insisted: I had come to an impasse in the book, writer's block, the work had stalled, and Solomon himself had ordered me to get in touch with him the moment any difficulty arose. The advisor sighed, looked again at the schedule.

"I'll see if I can squeeze you in. But you'll have, like, fifteen minutes, okay? Fifteen minutes. Make it quick."

We entered and there was Solomon sitting on his throne, receiving foreign dignitaries. Without making a scene, without excusing myself, I climbed the steps, the lions shaking their carved wooden heads in disapproval, and whispered in his ear:

"You have to see Mikol, Solomon. The poor woman is dying. It's her last request."

He frowned. "Mikol? I know who she is, but I'm not quite remembering..."

Before he could ask the scribe to bring her file, something that would take even more time, I quickly explained that she was one of the first concubines in his harem, the one that—

Oh yes, now he remembered. But it wasn't a happy memory. "She's the one who cheated on me," he said somberly. "The one who went behind my back with half the world."

"She's dying," harshly, sternly, I insisted. "This isn't time for payback, Solomon."

He began to say that he couldn't at the moment, that he was going to send his doctor to see her.

"No!" I yelled, startling the visitors, who didn't know what was going on. "She doesn't want the doctor. She wants you."

Still he resisted. He was unable to abandon the throne room right then, the people there were very important; a treaty was about to be signed that very day, a treaty that involved the touchy subject of the country's foreign debt.

That really lit a fire in me. Poor Mikol in agony and the guy she'd given her life to was busy with hearings and ceremonies. Furious, I was adamant: "Nope. You go there now."

"Tomorrow," he whispered. "I promise tomorrow..."

"Today. If you don't go today, I swear I'll walk away from all that book shit and leave you. You'll never see me again."

He sighed. "Okay. Tonight."

"No. Right now."

"No can do. In the afternoon, I'll go. First thing in the afternoon."

It was almost midnight when he made his way to Mikol's stall. Already in a coma, she never knew it. A week later she died.

Mikol's death went entirely unnoticed at court. Half a dozen women attended the burial, including a sister of hers and me. Solomon failed to grace us with his presence. He was very busy in those days. He was awaiting an important visitor. Important visitors weren't unheard of in his schedule, but this one was exceptional, so much so that in the palace corridors it was all people talked about; even the stern elders made remarks about it. Do you know who's coming here? they would ask me, wide-eyed.

I didn't know and I didn't want to know. Consumed by my pain, I refused to think of anything else. Mikol's absence was unbearable and, to make matters worse, I could not confide my loss to anyone. Among the women of the harem she was not very well known; the elderly women from The Retreat remembered her, but when they did, it was with jealousy: She may have been the king's little sweetheart, but she turned her nose up at us. My sadness was such that I thought about returning to my village in search of refuge with my family. But more than likely they wouldn't understand. A concubine died? So what? Aren't there two hundred ninety-nine left over? Besides, what did I care? I was a wife. I held a higher rank. If I'd happened to have maintained some type of relationship with the deceased, I ought to let it go; it was a bad look that could lead to suspicions of abomination.

The only person who was interested in Mikol's illness was another concubine, but for practical reasons. She wanted her bed. The one I have really sucks, she would say, it's killing my back. No sooner was Mikol buried than she took possession of her new bed with the satisfaction of one who plants her flag in conquered territory.

With no one to talk to about my suffering, I doubled down on my work. But I couldn't help but notice the unusual hustle and bustle going on about the palace: people cleaning, repairing things, bringing in furniture, rugs, lamps. I figured it was tied to the anticipated visit, and I asked the harem overseer who was about to arrive. She looked at me in shock, as if I had come from another planet.

"But you don't know? Get your head out of the clouds. Why, the Queen of Sheba, girl! She's coming for a visit!"

"And who is the Queen of Sheba?" I asked, truly uninterested: Kings and queens came and went on a daily basis. I could no longer keep up with memorizing the names of the strange countries they came from. She looked at me again, stunned by my degree of ignorance. How could I, a cultured woman handpicked by Solomon to write an important book, not know who the Queen of Sheba was? Well, I didn't know, could she possibly explain it to me?

"Of course I can," she said, happy for the chance to provide a footnote that might make it into the future book: "Details about the arrival of the Queen of Sheba had previously been announced by the harem overseer, the well-informed lady..."

She was a sovereign from a legendary country whose location no one knew for sure: it was in Arabia according to some, in Africa according to others. She was famous for her beauty and her audacity and her riches. For some time now, her desire had been to meet Solomon, whose renown as a wise man had even traveled so far as to reach her. Her tour had the exclusive goal of coming to see the king, a visit that would probably be for a prolonged time. It was no surprise that the women of the harem were quite frankly upset at the news. Competition for Solomon's bed was already intense; the arrival of a foreign queen would complicate things. Apparently, she came in search of wise counsel, like other rulers; but did her stated purpose perhaps mask ulterior motives, a politico-sexual alliance? Whatever the case, the king would have to invest considerable time with his guest and this, at the very least, would force him to spend even less time with the women of the harem, stirring up heightened competition that pushed the limits of tolerability.

As for me, I didn't take part in their worries. Mourning the death of Mikol, I refused to engage in palace gossip. What's more, under constant pressure from the elders, I had to focus on the text. At that moment we were working on a tormented and difficult character: Saul, the first king of Israel. There he was, grappling with the classic binomial of power and war—cruel war, in the case of the Amalekites, for example, that resulted in the massacre of men, women, and children. Cruelties had been a dime a dozen up till then—the scrolls piled on my table were full of them. What was new in our history was a ruler who suffered from depression. I was glad he was depressed, that he fit in with tortured groups like the ugly, the cancerous, and the maimed. In my eyes, that made him more human. It was something that I now craved: to be more human, to turn the ressentiment born of my ugliness and my latest pain of losing Mikol into quiet acceptance, into wisdom. Wisdom—but not like Solomon's, which to me seemed more like cleverness than anything. What I sought was genuine, authentic wisdom that could only be fully grasped in elaborate suffering. The fact that Saul sought out comfort in music moved me. In the moments of my greatest suffering I, too, hummed the songs that my mother and the village women sang from my childhood. When I began to write about Saul, I believed he was on the path to holiness.

But holiness would not come. And it would not come to him because of his tragic, toxic relationship with David. Those men, I thought, could have learned a thing or two from Ruth and Naomi. But maybe friendship was too simple of a thing for people so complicated. Saul loved and hated David at the same time; he tried to kill him but also gave him his daughter in marriage. That he'd consulted the Witch of Endor, and with her help heard the voice of Samuel, his deceased mentor, was proof to me of how stunted he was emotionally. Now there was a man I could comfort and charm with my stories, much more so than self-sufficient Solomon. Unfortunately, I had arrived two kings too late.

With David, Saul's successor, we were finally in the recent past, a past of which the elders could give personal testimony. They no longer needed to consult scrolls; they simply had to let their own reverent memories flow. Such memories spoke of an exceptionally attractive man, a musician, poet, warrior, and lover of women. They spoke of his unforgettable fight with the giant Goliath in the battle against the Philistines. They spoke of him building Jerusalem, where he had brought the Arc of the Covenant. They spoke of his victories over the Philistines, the Edomites, the Moabites, the Ammonites, and the Canaanites, which resulted in considerable expansion of the kingdom.

At the same time, they couldn't conceal less glorious episodes, like the tragic revolt of his son Absalom, who by the way, died fighting against his father. Then there was the very disturbing story of Bathsheba, which they narrated in a constrained way, without looking at each other or at me. And for good reason. The way David got rid of Uriah, all because he was in love with Uriah's wife, Bathsheba, was simply repulsive: He sent his officer to occupy a dangerous post on the front lines where, as expected, the man went MIA. God, who is all-seeing, punished him for his ignominy: The couple's first son died. But the second one lived and became king. King Solomon.

With that story everything suddenly became clear to me. I understood Solomon, his desire for women, especially for beautiful women. And I also identified a fissure in the solid edifice of his emotional stability. Did he not feel haunted by the shadow of his brother, by a shadow lurking in the palace attic, hiding behind the curtains of the Temple, in the penumbra of his bedroom, the bedroom where he had inexplicably lost his erection? Shadows are ubiquitous; they can hide anywhere, in anything, in a plant, carnivorous or otherwise, in a mammal, in a bird: The crow in the garden that cawed mockingly or the pigeon that never flew and stared down everyone with its black-eyed-pea eyes—they had what it took to bear his brother's suffering soul. Maybe that's why he'd studied birdtalk, to interrogate each crow, each pigeon, asking them, What do you want from me, bro? It wasn't my fault the hand of God smote you, not my fault you were chosen to atone for the sins of our parents.

But, and here was the heart of the matter, Solomon did have a reason to feel guilty. His brother had died so that he could live—and live lavishly in riches and luxury, with seven hundred wives and three hundred concubines. When Solomon had asked God to give him wisdom, he wasn't solely wanting to understand others. He was hoping to understand himself. More than that, he wanted to understand the past—a complicated task and massive undertaking for which I had been mobilized. The book wasn't just a would-be cultural monument, it would be a lighthouse in time, an answer to the riddle. Solomon needed to find meaning in the historical trajectory of which he was an integral part. If he could prove that a long process starting with the first man and woman culminated in him, if he could show that in him was concentrated the misery and greatness of the past, virtue and sin, right and wrong, if he could prove himself to be a cluster of contradictions—but also a human being struggling to be just, to judge others and himself fairly, to hand over a disputed baby to the right mother—maybe then the soul of his brother would leave him in peace and go off in search of his much-deserved rest in the Valley of the Shadow of Death. That was, well, the true objective of the text I was working on: history as exorcism. Little did Solomon know I was trying to infiltrate the narrative, that I wanted to substitute, between the lines, the specter of his disgruntled brother with the specter of my sexual frustration. A lot of stuff between the lines, eh? Lots of stuff.

Hauntings are contagious. Having written about Solomon's dead brother, I began to feel, there in the palace, the presence of his soul—tormented like my own. He spied on me, like Solomon spied: behind a pile of scrolls, from under the table where I worked. Except that his invisible presence didn't scare me. Quite the contrary, it fascinated me. We had lots in common. I, too, wandered through life in search of my place in it. I, too, felt scorned, marginalized. His gentle soul, which from this life departed all too soon, I wanted that soul. If I could lure it in, if I could absorb it inside myself, if I could incorporate it, well then . . . it would be a win-win. First, the pleasure of betraying Solomon; it wouldn't be about tangible pleasures of the flesh, the pleasure that Mikol had enjoyed, above all with the shepherd boy (what was he up to?), but a virtual pleasure, perhaps even more refined. Besides all that, I would gain special power over Solomon. He would see in me not wife number seven hundred and one, not the ugly scribe, but—literally—a soulmate. At first he would draw near with apprehension, fearing the fatal attraction, but I, with the authority that would now be vested in me due to my status as soul-bearer of his dead brother, I would absolve him and, as living proof, consent to him making love to me.

Incorporating the brother's suffering soul would be no easy feat. To do it, I would first have to establish contact with the afterlife (maybe Mikol, a recent arrival, could help me: Hello, hello, Mikol, could you find Solomon's deceased brother for me there? I'd like to offer him my mortal coil here on Earth. Tell him it's not an offer to take lightly; you can attest to my ugly face but let him know I have a nice body. He won't be totally disappointed). Then I would need to attract his elusive spirit and imprison it inside me. But how to go about it? Running naked through the corridors, in hopes of catching his errant ectoplasm in my mouth, in my nostrils, in my vagina? It was complicated, to say the least. As a wife, I had certain privileges, but I couldn't run around in my birthday suit. Oh, if only the Witch of Endor could help me. But the witch had died a long time ago and, as far as I knew, she left behind neither a successor nor an instruction manual on the matter. The sole proprietor of all wisdom, even occult wisdom, was now Solomon, who would never help me in my undertaking. So I decided to postpone my plan to capture the specter. Especially since at the moment the king didn't seem to be very concerned with the memory of his dead brother. The whole palace was in thrall to a party vibe. The Queen of Sheba was coming. Jerusalem, all dressed up for the occasion, was prepared to receive her. In Solomon's chamber next to mine, there was a new bed with a luxurious silk canopy, which was an ominous sign of much fuckery to come.

I was working one morning when out of nowhere sounded dozens of trumpets. I ran to the window. A caravan was arriving at the palace. And what a caravan it was! More than two hundred camels decked out in colorful finery. The one up front, a huge animal, carried a tent like the one I had traveled in, but much bigger and much fancier—the Queen of Sheba's tent. Solomon and his retinue were already there waiting. The camel kneeled, the tent curtains parted, and out stepped the sovereign.

Oh. My. God. What a beautiful woman! Absolutely beautiful. A tall black woman, slender, with the most stunning features: large eyes, sensual, full lips—absurdly beautiful. Next to her the seven hundred wives and three hundred concubines were little more than sad specimens (me, not even worth mentioning). The envious looks I spotted bore witness to their embarrassing contrast. Their penetrating stares were searching for something, some defect in her face and body; but they found nothing, because we were in the presence of absolute perfection. Naturally, her complexion caught our attention; we all had olive skin, but none of us was black. And so? With pride the queen could gloat, Sh'chorah ani ve'navah, b'not Yerushalayim, I am black and I am beautiful, O daughters of Jerusalem. And the daughters of Jerusalem, and any daughters from anywhere else for that matter, would have to keep their resentful yaps shut.

The king stepped forward, beaming. He made a small speech saying it was a historic day, that the queen's visit added to the tally of blessings that God had bestowed upon his kingdom: "Our reputation spreads throughout the known world. Our Temple brings visitors from all over. Soon..."

Dramatic pause.

"Soon all this will be coronated with a work of greater importance, not a material work but an intellectual one, which will forever leave its mark on the history of humanity. And I am made happy by the fact that the rollout of this work coincides with the visit of the Queen of Sheba, who has traveled from so far to honor us."

The revelation created undeniable suspense: What was the king talking about? What intellectual work could it be? Everyone was intrigued, me more than anyone. Was the king talking about the book I was working on? Was he attempting to honor a stranger, no matter how important, with the sweat of my brow (and the sweat of others)? Or was it simply a publicity stunt, intended to bring attention to the launch of the work? Whatever the reason, what was certain was that I had not been consulted, and that activated my bitchface. I decided that the first chance I got, I would call him out and ask him what game he was playing.

When the ceremony ended, Solomon invited the queen to rest in the chambers that had been prepared for her. The two walked down the palace corridors, everyone else going out of their way to catch a glimpse of her and her grace and her beauty, and she knocking all their socks off when they did. Unable to stand it anymore, I went to my room. Where the manuscripts were waiting for me. What did I, the ugly one, want? For me there was neither fanfare nor smiles. For me, only work. Work that, by the looks of it, would be used by Solomon to enhance his international prestige.

The same night Solomon held a banquet that would go down in royal history;

delicacies without end, prepared by cooks from faraway lands, a thousand varieties of wine, exotic fruits . . . in short, a wild time. I looked on from the door because, of the wives, only the hundred oldest had been invited—the explanation being that there was no room for all of them. A lie. The real reason was that the older wives, because of their seniority, were the least resentful.

The queen was poised to return the favor; at the snap of her finger nearly fifty slaves weighed down by her offerings entered the hall.

And those were some offerings. God, did she know her stuff! Rare and expensive perfumes. Precious stones. Gold—four thousand kilos of gold, as I later found out. Which practically erased the whole foreign debt problem. Solomon probably had enough loot to do some final touch-ups on the Temple, fund better equipment for his army, buy more concubines. The price of gold was up on the international market and, with his coffers filled, Solomon no longer had reason to go in search of it in the mysterious mines of Ophir, which were God knows where: in Africa, some said, in the tropical lands of the Amazons, others claimed. Now, all of that in exchange for some measly advice? Or was he forming a new alliance with the queen, reaching out to a new and promising frontier that would span from the Middle East to Africa?

Whatever the case, the illustrious guest was already running circles around the harem women. All of them combined had not yielded to the Crown, in tributes and other favors, half of what she was packing. In beauty, it was the same story: All together they didn't hold a candle to the fascinating woman.

The consequences were not long in coming. Solomon simply chose to ignore his wives and concubines—they would have to remain in quarantine until the end of her visit.

But he sent for me. To tell me that, as stated to the visitors at the reception, he intended to gift the queen a copy of the history I was writing. Several scribes were already working round the clock to reproduce what I had written—but it was also necessary that I finish the description of David's kingdom and get on with the part about Solomon. There I would include the description of the queen's visit, mentioning the four thousand kilos of gold along with everything else. It was to be the final chapter, the gold clasp on the narrative (metaphoric gold, of course; the real deal was already in the royal treasury). I therefore needed to pick up the pace of my work.

I didn't say a word. What could I say? I was charged with a task, I had to fulfill it. Pleasures of the flesh were reserved for the Queen of Sheba. Who was beautiful. Who had offered four thousand kilos of gold to the king. I had no claim to stake. So I went back to my manuscript.

I was back at it when there came a knock at my door. It was a slave girl. She brought a message from the women: They wanted me to go to the harem to talk to them. About what, she wasn't sure. But it was urgent.

I didn't have to think hard to come to the conclusion that their request had something to do with the queen's visit. What's more, it was definitely something serious; a bomb was about to be dropped. Despite my race against the clock—David's story was proving tricky—I managed to sneak off.

As I had anticipated, I found them on the brink of war, worked up into a frenzy over what they called Solomon's scorn. Ever since the black woman's arrival, said one, we don't get our turn. Another added: This king, wise? The guy has the wool pulled over his eyes by the first foreigner who shows up at his doorstep. There was even one who brought up that witchcraft was a common practice in Africa: a love potion secretly added to Solomon's wine and, *poof*, the drooling idiot fell in love.

After talking it over, they had decided to unleash a protest movement and they wanted me to take the helm; after all, having a certain level of influence with the king (at least that's how they imagined it), I could approach him with the harem's demands.

Maybe I would have accepted the charge months earlier, and with gusto. Now, however, everything had changed, and I was not the same person. I didn't feel the least bit of desire to go picking a fight. Jaded? Resigned? I don't know. The truth is I didn't have the stomach for a fight. But I also didn't want to abandon them. I mean, they were my partners in crime, and if they were going through a rough patch, it was my duty to help them.

I asked what they had in mind and it was, of course, a sex strike: a pact in which they would refuse to go to bed with Solomon.

"But that's exactly what he wants," I said.

They looked at me, shocked. What? A women's strike wouldn't upset the king? I said no, that sex-wise Solomon was probably getting more than his fill with his visitor. It was therefore inevitable that he would spend his time fooling around with her. The real question was whether he was contemplating prolonging their union. Would he consider turning his political alliance into full-on marriage? And if that happened, to what role would the wives and concubines be relegated?

Uncomfortable questions, which left the women in a state—especially since I didn't have any answers for them.

"Do you mean there's nothing we can do?" asked one of them.

"I didn't say that," I replied. "I said you will have to use your head. And the first thing is finding out what Solomon's intentions are with this woman."

Yes, that seemed sensible to them, except they didn't know how to act. Again, they asked for—they asked for, no, they implored—my help. I could help them. For one simple reason: The queen was lodged in the room next to mine. Every night Solomon went there. His pretext might be to provide counsel about the extraction of foreign resources, but the goings-on were something else entirely: that familiar symphony of moaning, gasping, screaming even. They were a loud couple (and why do it in silence if they answered to no one?). During the initial days I did whatever I could to ignore them, plugging my ears with cotton, trying to concentrate on my work—at the time I was focused on the description of the Temple, with all the details the king demanded, and they were not few in number. At the women's request, I began to press my ear against the wall and listen in on them. My work would have to wait. I wanted to know what the king and queen were saying.

To my surprise, they talked a lot. Before fucking, while fucking, after fucking. It wasn't your everyday dirty talk between lovers, the woman screaming, Put it in deeper, the man saying, You like that, don't you? Yeah, you know you want it. No. To my surprise, and profound envy, their dialogue was very classy—and in verse. "Cover me with the kisses of your mouth," she would say in the Hebrew she had learned just for her trip, and then: "Your caresses are sweeter than wine and more aromatic than perfume is your name; that is why young women fall for you."

(And later, I might add, they end up in your harem, bursting at the seams with rage.)

Solomon, for his part, would join in with allusive comparisons to power and riches: "I compare you to the horses of Pharoah's chariots, my love. Lovely is your face, lovely your neck. We shall make you golden earrings, with silver filigree."

(With gold she provided. Silver she provided. What a douche!)

At times they would set aside their fetish for grandeur and exchange more ecological comparisons, so to speak. She was "the lily among the thorns," he a gazelle (gazelle?!) who went "frolicking through the hills." He brought it down to anatomical levels: "Your hair is like a flock of goats" (goats, hmm. Had he taken sex ed with the shepherd boy?). "Your teeth are like a flock of sheep."

Sometimes the poetic license he ad-libbed was a shameful lie. At one point he told her: "Seventy are my queens / eighty my concubines / and numerous my maidens. / Nevertheless, only one is my dove . . ."

In other words, his seven hundred wives had been reduced to seventy, a reduction of more than ninety percent. The concubines suffered less of a loss, from three hundred to eighty. Which made his disregard for his spouses even worse. Now, could it be that that fool of a queen didn't know? Everyone knew she'd been taken in by the king's supposed wisdom, but was that cause for losing all her faculty of reason? Anybody could see that the number of harem women was much higher than what Solomon mentioned in his aberrant assertion of matrimonial goods—how could she fall for it? Maybe because he didn't give her time, piling on the flattery. "Your belly is like a goblet, may it never be empty of wine . . ." Followed by giggles and moans and smut, lots of smut.

That's what I heard, or what I thought I heard, because at times they spoke in hushed voices and I practically had to guess what they were saying. I wrote everything down, filling parchment after parchment. A real consolation prize—instead of knocking boots, pencil-pushing—but it would serve my objectives. I intended, at the right moment, to present it as evidence to back my accusation: "Do you deny that, on the night from the 16th to the 17th, while lying with that woman, you compared her belly to a goblet, in a clear act of indecency and also, but no less important, under the heavy influence of alcoholic beverages?"

But they could care less about possible accusations. The Queen of Sheba, for the time being, was the belle of the ball. No sooner had she installed herself in the palace than she infiltrated it with her entire court as well, including her slaves; they spent all day in the palace corridors, laughing, cutting up, singing. Exotic people, but not totally unfriendly.

☀

There was a guy in their ranks who struck me as odd, sinister even. The man hid beneath a cloak that covered his face and left only his eyes exposed—and they were some eyes. In them was a savage spark, raving almost, that gave me the chills. And worse of all was that he was always staring at me. Coinkydink or not, I definitely kept catching him hanging around the palace corridors, near my room. After a bit of sleuthing, I learned that the man was not one of the queen's subjects; he was a Jew who'd approached the caravan leaders in the southern desert. Warning them of the danger on those misleading roads, full of bandits, the man offered to lead them to Jerusalem, an offer that was eagerly accepted. He was supposed to guide them on their return also. It was all very plausible, but—why did the dude fixate on me so insistently? Even the elders had taken note. My ex-creep, the one who'd surprised me with an erection, ironically told me (and not out of jealousy) that the guy was probably in love with me.

I had to clear this all up. One evening, around dusk, I found the hooded man alone in the corridor. Now or never, I thought. Working up the nerve, I approached him. He didn't walk off; in fact, he seemed to have been waiting for this moment. For an instant, we stood there looking at each other, he with his fixed, hypnotic gaze. Until I couldn't stand it anymore.

"Come on, man, what do you want with me?"

He didn't immediately respond. When he did, it was in a raspy, almost imperceptible voice: "You know who I am."

The shepherd boy. Oh my God, it was the shepherd boy! My first reaction was to rejoice: So you're alive, that's great, and I didn't hear from you; yeah, I suffered lots, but luckily you got away, that's swell.

He, on the other hand, didn't manifest any enthusiasm or joy. I'd presumed he was going to hug me or at least give me an enthusiastic hi. But no, he remained stock-still, staring at me. Which profoundly unnerved me. What did his stillness mean, and that crazy look? He had undoubtedly changed, a lot. The boy who used to dart along mountain trails, the boy who grazed his goats (and who humped them), the boy who took my sister to the cave, the boy who was prepared to take my letter to my father—that wasn't the same boy standing here before me. He was odd, different, a guy who inspired irrepressible fear in me. Why? What had made him change? Sure, he'd had a rough go of it, the stoning, his banishment, the fight with the soldiers, the loss of his arm—which, by the way, explained the cloak: He didn't want people to see his deformity. However, none of that explained his callousness and detachment; above all, it didn't explain the raving gleam I saw in his eyes. They accused me, as if I were responsible for his suffering.

I took a deep breath, then: "What's your deal?" I asked.

He hesitated, looked around. "I can't talk here. Can we go to a more secluded place?"

I said yes, that we could talk in my room.

"So you have a room in the palace," he observed ironically. "A room all to yourself. All right then, lead the way."

We went. In the corridor we crossed paths with one of the elders, who looked at us suspiciously. Let him suspect all he wants, I'd had it up to here. I needed to talk to the shepherd boy to know precisely what was going on, because I knew now that something was up.

We went in, I closed the door. Using the stump of his arm, he struggled to take off his heavy garb.

I was dealing with a handsome man, not the boy I had known in the past. Yet the expression on his face—scarred from the stoning he had received—was bitter, savage even. Bitterness like his I had never seen. But he wasn't the type to go chafing with resentment.

He looked around, checking to make sure we were alone, that no one could hear us. And then, drawing near to me, he said, in a confidential tone: "I'm here on a mission. I'm not just the queen's guide for her caravan. That was a cover to get into the palace. My mission is something else entirely. My mission is revenge. Holy revenge."

Only then did I catch a glimpse of the knives he carried at his waist. A chill ran down my spine: two knives, one on each side, curved knives, the knives of an assassin. The man was serious. Apparently someone would pay for his lost arm.

He read my mind and smiled bitterly. "You must think it's personal, that I aim to take out my revenge on the king's soldiers. You're mistaken. If you must know, losing my arm was a blessing in disguise. A divine message that forced me to think long and hard about my life, my destiny. Who was I before all this? You know very well: a depraved sinner. I mean, think about it: I had sexual relations with goats."

A constrained pause, but, since he'd already begun, he might as well get to the end. "I was a master goatfucker. I'd sneak up behind them, singing softly the song that I knew buttered them up, and then, *bing, bang, boom*! I knew them; one, two, three, there was no limit to my abomination. Poor goats, poor little guys, they paid the price for my horniness. And with your sister it was the same: abomination on top of abomination. But in her case, it was because she begged for it, not because I insisted. I'm sorry to say it, but she is as much of a sinner as I am. I thought she loved me, but no, she was all about dirty, vile sex. And I paid the price."

I listened. Horrified? No, not quite. Fascinated? No, not that either. I simply listened to him. And I didn't know what to make of his surprise confession.

"Your father had me stoned and banished," he went on. "But the punishment didn't stick. I didn't learn my lesson. Because he was just getting back at me, you know? He wasn't acting in the name of righteousness, he was acting in his own name, punishing me for tarnishing his reputation. I didn't change at all. I left our land, came to Jerusalem, and continued on the road to perdition. Once you start, as you know, it's hard to stop. And I'm not just talking the miserable gals I banged along the way. No! Even here at the palace I had a lover, an old concubine ... she saw me one time, from her window, and fell in love with me. She would escape the harem to be with me. And do you think I was grateful to this woman? No. I took what she gave. I took jewels from her, I took money ..."

Poor Mikol. Poor, poor Mikol.

"And that's when I ran into you. I'd gone days without seeing the woman, which was a disaster. Without her help I would starve. I had to beg for alms. It occurred to me to sit against the palace wall and play my flute—she knew about my skill. But you showed up, not her, and then you asked me to take the letter to your father. Do you know why I accepted? Because I was so excited to see you. I was excited because—"

He cut himself off and stood there, staring at me in a strange way. He had something to tell me, something that was very important, but it bothered him—and it bothered me too. Suddenly, everything I had felt for him was coming back to me; and this time, it seemed, it was something he too felt. Hence his internal conflict. But he wouldn't give in. He took a deep breath.

"Leave it be. One day, if the day comes, we will talk about it. Right now I want to tell you about what happened. Like I was saying, that's when the soldiers jumped me. And that's what you know. They wanted me to hand over the letter you gave me. They got pushy and I defended myself as best I could, but it wasn't a fair fight, sword against knife. I lost my arm, got it cut off by their commander. I almost died, but luckily a charitable soul cared for me. Maimed, I again wandered the streets, begging and starving. But even so, as incredible as it might seem, I still hadn't learned my lesson. I was full of hate, yes, but blind hate without direction. Finally, after much wandering, I made it to the mountain, our mountain—make no mistake, it wasn't chance but divine intervention. There, in the ancient cave of abominations, in the cave where your father used to cheat and where I would seduce goats and, later, your sister, I found the Master of Justice and his disciples."

He looked at me.

"Master of Justice. Never heard of him, huh? You will. From here on out, you will know his name. The Master of Justice was like your father: a rich patriarch, a powerful man, but a whoremonger. Schtupped like a wild man, mistreated the people of his tribe. Like me, he was punished by Solomon, got arrested for failing to pay his taxes. He was in jail for three years, here in Jerusalem. And then it happened: One night Solomon's brother, a kid with big, sad eyes, appeared to him in his dreams. The dead man said he couldn't rest in peace because of the sins of the arrogant king. I have a mission for you, he said. It's up to you to cleanse our sinful land of its depravity. The Master of Justice then went about the country preaching and attracting a following of disciples—a small group, because, as you know, few are chosen. By the grace of God I joined this group when I first heard the Master's words, wise words that changed my life."

"And what does he say?" I asked.

"He says," his eyes bright, eyebrows arched, "he says that the end is nigh. The signs are right in front of our noses. Even you can tell: Solomon, our king, does not respect the word of the Lord. His harem is full of foreigners: Moabites, Ammonites, Edomites, Hittites, not to mention the Queen of Sheba, that black woman he sleeps with every night. Solomon follows Astarte, the Great Goddess of the pagans, the Great Prostitute for our people, the deity that the powers of the underworld bow down to. Solomon built a temple to the gods of the Ammonites. And to finance that whole abomination, the people wail under his tax burden. Is this our wise king? Answer me, is his wisdom fit for a king?"

Without waiting for my answer, he went on, more and more frenetic than ever: "Behold, we, the Warriors of Righteousness, under the command of the Master of Justice, are already making preparations. For now, like I said, we are few. But soon, multitudes will join us. And then we shall fight the final battle. When that happens, rivers will flow with blood throughout the land, washing away all sin and abomination."

I have to say, I was impressed—and alarmed. There was no way around it; the guy was ready to kill and be killed. One doubt troubled me: What was he doing in the palace? Why had he accompanied the Queen of Sheba? He said it was a mission. I asked him what mission, but he refused to tell me. With a pale smile and declining my help, he went to put on his cloak.

"I've said what I have to say. The rest is for you to find out, when the time comes. And I can promise you, the time is near."

Now a bit more leisurely—which contrasted drastically with his previous rant—he started walking around the room. He looked at the scrolls on the shelves, wanted know what they were about. I told him I was writing a book for Solomon.

"A book," he sighed. "Yes, I knew one day you would write a book. You were always smart. Smarter than your sister—smarter and kinder. Thinking it over, I—"

He paused once more, turned to look at the manuscript. And in a tone that attempted to sound neutral but expressed unmistakable torment, he said: "I imagine this book is very important to him."

"It is. Very important. He says it's as important as the Temple. He even intends to give a copy to the Queen of Sheba."

He smiled ironically and put the manuscript away on the shelf. "That's why he keeps you locked up here. So that you will write a book for the Queen of Sheba. It's another one of his abominations. But it will come to an end, I promise you that. Quicker than you think."

Again with the riddles. What did he mean by all of this? Before I could ask him, he said he had to go, his absence would raise suspicions. He took me by the hand. There was affection in his gesture, tender affection. He asked me not to tell anyone about our conversation. He opened the door with a smile—which carried something sinister but somehow still expressed the shepherd boy's shyness—and vanished into the shadows of the corridor.

I fell back onto the bed. I was so confused and so frightened that I didn't know what to think. But I knew I had to find out what had brought the shepherd boy to the palace, and soon. A mission, he'd said. But what sort of solo mission could the guy be on? Might it be that he intended, for example, to do his own preaching like the prophets of old, shouting, The end is nigh, the end is upon us? No. Giving speeches wasn't his style. His style was different. What he had in mind was something else. So what was it?

It suddenly occurred to me: an attempt. Of course. How had I not thought of that before? An attempt. Carefully planned, by the looks of it. His encounter with the queen's caravan, which definitely was no coincidence, gave him the chance to sneak into the palace disguised as a guide. And now he was here, armed and ready for action.

But an attempt against whom? Against one of the women he'd talked so angrily about, a Moabite, an Ammonite, an Edomite, a Hittite? What good would it be to kill one woman, since the harem had so many? Or maybe it was someone in the court—like the head of security, the one who had cut off his arm? But it didn't seem like he was particularly angry at the soldiers who had attacked him and who, at the end of the day, had been following orders.

No, his target was someone else.

Solomon. He was after the king. When I came to this realization, a chill ran down my spine. Solomon? The king? Still, it made sense. It made sense according to the shepherd boy's logic. After all, the king was the supreme sinner—and the ultimate traitor—the man who had used his wisdom granted by God to glorify himself, to live lavishly in splendor and luxury. That he had built the Temple apparently didn't matter. The Temple was the domain of the high clergy, united with the king in their mutual interests. No, the Temple did not nullify the king's transgressions of divine law. The Master of Justice had decided Solomon needed to be cut down to size. And the former shepherd boy was his instrument for doing so.

One thing, however, intrigued me: Why tell me all this? Why did he make me his confidant? There was only one explanation: He considered me an ally. The way he saw it, I was like him, a victim: victim of my father, of Solomon. Locked up in my room, writing a book—I was a slave to the king, yearning for freedom.

But was I a slave? That was the question I asked myself in that moment. A sublime question; The answer that I gave myself would determine how I would act. Was I a slave? Was I under the heel of Solomon?

No. I was not a slave. Nor did I long for freedom. If I lived in captivity, I had gotten used to my captivity; I mean, I'd made Solomon's project my project. Had life been so bad for me? Maybe. Since coming to the palace, I had been subjected to countless humiliations. And if I wanted to blame Solomon for my humiliation I could.

But I wouldn't do it. Because of the text, the history I was writing. The text consoled me, it sheltered me, gave me meaning in life. Through the text I could communicate with Solomon. And it wasn't a message of hate that I would transmit to him. I knew that deep down he was a human being, a person like anyone else. He wasn't the best but he wasn't the worst. And that's why he didn't deserve the punishment they had in store for him—which would solve nothing and might not even work. I wasn't even sure what the shepherd boy was planning, but I knew it would end in disaster—for him, probably. Only his fanaticism could lead him to believe that he could sneak into the palace and kill the king. The likelihood of him injuring Solomon was slim; the guards would chop him to pieces before he could even make his move. Regardless, it was dangerous, mostly for him, but also, more remotely, for the monarch.

There was only one way to avoid disaster. I had to let Solomon know. The problem was no one knew where he and the queen were. I ran to the throne room, hoping he would be there holding court. He wasn't. I went to several of his rooms: not there either.

There was one place left: the bedchamber reserved for the Queen of Sheba. I ran there. The guards at the door immediately blocked my path. They confirmed that Solomon was inside, but he was not to be disturbed. Nervous, I explained that it was urgent, a matter of security. I argued, implored—to no avail. The king cannot be interrupted, they repeated. Orders are orders.

The whole thing had me livid—the king fucking, yet unwilling to give two fucks about anything else, not even about the danger he was in—but I didn't give up. I remembered the wall I could hear the two talking through. If I could hear them, then they could definitely hear me too. I went to my room, pressed my ear against the wall. Yes, they were in there all right, going at it again with their giggles and moans and dirty talk in verse: "Cover me with the kisses of your mouth, your belly is like a goblet," I knew the whole bit by heart.

"Solomon!" I called through the wall. "Solomon, open the door, I have to tell you something, it's urgent!"

No reply.

"Solomon, your throne is in jeopardy!"

His throne, in jeopardy? Apparently, he couldn't be bothered to stop screwing for such a trivial matter. His throne could go to hell, getting laid was better.

"Solomon, your life is in danger!"

Nothing. I lost my patience.

"Damn you, Solomon! Can't you stop screwing for one second and pay attention to something serious? For the love of God, where is your wisdom?"

There was now absolute silence from the other side. I could imagine Solomon whispering in the queen's ear: Don't worry, it's the ugly one, the woman is running out of ways to bust my balls, all because I refused to make love to her, so now she makes my life a living hell. Enraged, I grabbed a candleholder, a heavy bronze one, and began banging on the wall, sending thundering reverberations throughout the room. Nothing. And then I came undone and burst into tears. Solomon was so stupid that he would pay for his unbridled lust with his life. And there was nothing I could do about it.

Distressed, I sat still at my table, not knowing what to do or think. In front of me, manuscripts and parchment. Then, almost out of instinct, I grabbed the quill and began to write. It was my only option: writing, telling what had happened, bearing witness to these agonizing moments. A message for Solomon himself—if he survived. But it was also a message without an exact addressee, a message in a bottle thrown out into the sea of time. And what would the note contain? That even the wisest of men was a moron when sex was on the line. Getting my message out there was my mission, just like the mission the shepherd boy claimed he was on. Or like the mission the king believed himself to have completed when he built the Temple.

I began thusly: "King Solomon loved many foreign women."

And I stopped. Was that my message? It was more gossip than proclamation. Worse still, I wasn't saying anything new. If these walls could talk, they would have more to say about Solomon's dirty deeds than I could. What was I trying to do, file a complaint with the manager? And who was this manager? No, I had to go a different route. Leave the past behind and look to the future. I had to prophesy. Which I now realized wasn't that hard. What did prophets do if not detect in the present the embryo of things to come? It was like following a numerical sequence in which four would inevitably have to come after three. It was like beginning a text that, moved by its internal logic, auto-generated itself. When the prophet declared David's divine punishment, he wasn't fortune-telling, he was bean-counting. Of course the love between the king and Bathsheba would engender a child. Of course his child would be a symbol of his guilty passion. And of course his child would be sacrificed for it, like the animals sacrificed on the altar of the Temple.

Like the prophets, I was seeing with meridian clarity what would happen from here on out, not in the months or years to come, but in the coming centuries; a story that would give life to many books (and I even imagined a Greek name for those books, because that would be the lingua franca: Bible). Heartened by some mysterious force, my hand wrote and wrote in a fevered dream. As for the king, what would happen to a horndog who refused to get out of bed with a foreigner, preferring to fuck and recite the Song of Songs while others conspired to kill him? If he escaped their knives, he would keep building more and more shrines, and more and more sects would sprout up like mushrooms on manure, the filth of which he rolled in with women who had him wrapped around their fingers because of his weakness and vanity. His punishment was inevitable; a punishment that, following the general tone of the text, I would call divine: "And," I wrote, "the Lord was angry with Solomon, because he turned his heart from the Lord God of Israel who had commanded him not to follow after other gods. And he said to Solomon, 'Because you have done this, and have not kept my covenants and my statutes that I have commanded you, I will tear your kingdom from you and give it to one of your servants. However, for David your father's sake, I will not do it in your days, but I will tear it from the hands of your son.'"

Next I narrated how a revolt, taking place during the reign of Rehoboam, Solomon's son, divided the kingdom in two. I described those kingdoms torn by conflict; I spoke of the desperation of the prophets who, like me, tried to warn their rulers about the dangers of impiety. I anticipated the occupation of the region by great foreign powers, the last of which would be lord over a vast empire.

There I foresaw the great suffering and oppression of our people under the yolk of foreign rule, and in contrast, the cushy lives of the Temple priests and local rulers allied with the empire. The outcome of this situation could only be revolt—like the shepherd boy's—but also the birth of a new religion. In it, mysterious Jehovah would be replaced by Daddy-God, all-powerful, yes, but at the same time merciful. And there would be a Son, with whom the people would identify in their affliction; this Son, in human form, would preach love and justice, perform miracles, heal the sick—I was remembering the desperation of my friend Mikol, sick and without anyone to turn to. Naturally, he would be sacrificed by representatives of the empire and their local accomplices, but he would rise from among the dead and ascend to heaven. Oh, yeah, this Son would have a Mother, a feminine figure very different from Eve or even from the matriarchs (or from my absent mother), a Mother who would be the symbol of kindness, a feminine figure through whom the faithful could appeal to the Father and the Son. The Trinity would be complete with a Holy Ghost, symbolized by a bird—not the crows Solomon liked to talk to, but by a pure and innocent dove, very different from the palace pigeons, those bearers of tortured souls. Instead of the main Temple, with its costly sacrifices, thousands of temples would pop up, big and small, rich and poor, where everyone could attend with no problem, without offering sacrifices; priests would hear the people and absolve them of their sins, freeing them from our age-old guilt. The talk of Chosen People would come to an end; the new religion would attempt to conquer followers among all peoples. They would even put an end to distinguishing themselves from others with circumcision. In the shadow of this new religion, Solomon's glory would simply be eclipsed.

I finished writing at the crack of dawn. I looked at the scrolls, more than ten. What was I to do with them? Show the elders? No way. I could easily imagine their reactions: Shouting "Abomination! Abomination!" they would take the scrolls to Solomon, asking him to make an example of me. Especially since my job was pretty much finished. They no longer needed me.

No, I couldn't show them to anyone. I had to take a different approach: store the manuscripts in some sort of container, like a carefully sealed jar, and deposit it deep in a certain cave situated near a certain mountain. There the scrolls would wait for a long time, for centuries maybe. Until one day a shepherd boy, perhaps in search of his beloved lost goat, would discover the message there from the past. And then they would say, with admiration, that I was a wise woman. They would search for my bones, to put them on display for curious onlookers, but they would not find them. All that would remain of me would be in the text, in the salty residue of the tears I'd shed. But how would I get them to the cave? That's what I was thinking about when someone knocked on my door. It was the harem overseer. With an announcement.

"All are invited to appear in the great hall. It's urgent."

I felt dizzy. Urgent? Had it gone down? Had my prediction happened? I grabbed her by her garments, panic-stricken, What's going on, tell me, what happened to the king?

Startled and irritated, she looked at me. "What's all this about, woman?" she shouted, twisting away from me. "Have you lost your mind? Did you finally lose it? The king is fine; of course he is. Why wouldn't he be fine? He's the one summoning us. Everyone has to be there, the wives, the concubines, the courtiers, everyone. Come on, hurry up, you're late."

Solomon was okay. Oh, God, Solomon was fine. Thank you, God, my Cute Little God, thank you for saving his life. Thank you, God.

Calmer now, I asked what his summoning was all about.

She shook her head, smiling ironically. "So you don't know? You do live on another planet, don't you? The Queen of Sheba is leaving, we're going to give her a proper send-off. Girl, four thousand kilos of gold, that's not chump change. From now on, it's the good life for us."

She looked at me with surprise. "You're the one who's not okay. Look at your awful face. What's wrong?"

I gave her some random explanation: I hadn't slept well, lots of pain. "Menstrual cramps, you know how it is."

"I know. But that's no excuse to skip out, the king won't forgive you. Get it together and let's go. No more delays. The farewell is going to be quick, and it's about to start."

The farewell. Yes, I ought to be happy: The seductress was leaving. No more giggling, no more moaning, no more dirty talk in verse: Cover me with the kisses of your mouth. No more Your belly is like a goblet. It was over.

And then—still groggy, the wheels in my head slowly turning—I realized something that left me instantly frozen with fear. The farewell was the moment when the shepherd boy would execute his plan, the moment when his knife would rip into Solomon's flesh. I had to warn Solomon, without a moment to lose. How? I hadn't the slightest clue. However, one thing was certain: I couldn't lose my nerve. I had to keep a cool head. It would be no use running around yelling, Danger, danger, a crime is being committed! Given my reputation as the palace nut job, they would most likely detain me and lock me up in my room so that I wouldn't rain on the parade. No, I would have to go about it another way. But how? I didn't know yet. I would have to improvise in the moment.

I quickly got ready and followed the woman. The palace corridors were crowded, everyone hurrying toward the great hall. The harem women and the concubines didn't bother hiding their delight: Her departure is long overdue, they kept saying about the Queen of Sheba. The courtiers, who during the visit had also been blown off, shared in their satisfaction.

Much to my despair, the great hall was already full when I arrived. I had no way of getting close to the chairs reserved for Solomon and the Queen of Sheba. I tried to get through, alleging that, being short, I couldn't see a thing, but nobody made room for me: Who do you think you are? Just because you wrote that book doesn't mean you get special treatment. I decided to stand there in the doorway, straining on my tiptoes to see.

Suddenly I saw the shepherd boy. What a relief! I saw that, like me, he was by the door on the opposite end; he would have to get through lots of people to reach the king. But he was definitely up to something. I caught a glimpse of his hand gripping the knife under his cloak.

I desperately tried to catch his eye. Don't do it, was the silent message I tried to send him, you won't get what you're after, I know it won't work, I already wrote that Solomon will survive and I did not write in vain, a premonition took hold of me, a curtain to the future opened before my eyes. Don't do it, Solomon will pay for his mistakes, God is already taking care of it, you don't have to sacrifice your life for this harebrained scheme.

A man stood beside me, an armed man, sword at his waist. I instantly recognized him. He was the head of security, the officer who had cut off the shepherd boy's arm. The moment I'd been waiting for. Finally, a little help from God. Without hesitating, I pulled him aside.

"This is urgent," I whispered in his ear. "I've been reliably informed that there will be an attempt against the king. Right now."

He looked at me in disbelief. "An attempt? Against the king? An attempt against the king, here in the palace full of people—full of soldiers and guards? Impossible."

"It's true," I insisted. "The guide who led the caravan wants to kill Solomon. He's not just any guide. He's the man whose arm you cut off, and now he belongs to a band of fanatics. That's why he's here, to assassinate the king."

He still didn't believe me: The caravan guide was a quiet kid, didn't look like a bandit. Almost in tears now, I asked him to at least frisk the kid. He would find two knives at his waist.

"Okay fine," he finally grumbled. "I'll do it, but only because you're asking. Where is this guy?"

"There," I answered, pointing to the other side of the hall. But to my surprise and horror, the hooded figure was no longer there.

Now the officer was convinced I was serious: If the guy was no longer there, it was well within reason that he intended to attack the king before he entered the great hall. Calling two of his soldiers, he went running through the door. I breathed a sigh of relief while, at the same time and to the sound of fanfare, Solomon entered with the Queen of Sheba: he, spectacular in his royal mantle, she more gorgeous than ever. Everyone applauded politely. Smiling, the two took their seats in chairs surrounded by guards. Although he was unaware, the king was safe and sound. The shepherd boy would never be able to attack him there.

I breathed another sigh of relief. Man, that Solomon was a real son of a bitch, but could I help it if I liked him so much? If I was happy he had escaped? Despite his betrayal, despite giving the Queen of Sheba what I had always dreamed of, he was alive, and that was what mattered. On the other hand, I prayed for the shepherd boy to accept that his plan had been thwarted and to quietly walk away. Crisis averted, they wouldn't have to arrest him; if they did, he would definitely be executed for treason. And I didn't want that... No, I did not. I wanted him to live, the poor shepherd boy, the miserable shepherd boy, the shepherd boy who, like me, struggled to find his place in the world. But where could he be? Had he returned to the great hall? I stood on my tiptoes but was unsuccessful in getting a good look.

A sudden outburst of shouts came pouring in from the corridor: Fire! Fire! A burning smell immediately invaded the great hall. We all rushed outside in a panic, the women screaming their heads off.

The corridor was full of smoke. Puzzled, I took a few steps—and was intercepted by the harem overseer.

"It's in your room," she shouted. "The fire is in your room."

We ran there. Sure enough, everything was in flames. Everything: the furniture, my clothes, my manuscripts. The entire history I'd written and all my foresight. Jehovah. Adam and Eve. Cain and Abel. Abraham, Isaac, and Jacob. Moses. Saul and David. Solomon and the Temple. The Queen of Sheba. The Father, the Son, and the Holy Ghost. The Mother. Miracles and curses, rewards and punishments, laughter and tears, commandments, dreams, visions, prophecies. Everything turning to ash. Nothing would survive, not even the queen's copy, which I'd just revised. It was supposed to be given to her upon her departure. I bent down, grabbed a fragment of burned parchment. "Then they asked," was written there. Who asked? And what did they ask? Whom did they ask? What was the answer? I didn't know what it was about. I would never know. Let some other man, or woman, reconstruct the text. My job here was done.

Amidst all the smoke, I spotted the shepherd boy in the clutches of two soldiers: One held him by the arm, the other by the stump of his arm. Having lost his cloak, he was half naked and bleeding from several wounds. But he had his head held high with an expression of triumph—desperate triumph, but triumph. The officer I had warned of the possible attempt was also there with the men.

"It was him," he roared. "He set fire to the scrolls. He wanted to sow confusion to get to the king."

No. That wasn't it. It wasn't the king the shepherd boy was after. I saw that now. Maybe killing him had been his original objective, the initial mission assigned to him by the Master of Justice—up until last night. He'd changed his mind after visiting my room. It wasn't about the king anymore. It was about the royal manuscript. No, it was about me. I could tell the moment when the soldiers escorting him passed me and our eyes met. I was thinking of you when I did this, his sad, soft eyes said to me, to set you free. Poor shepherd boy, my dear shepherd boy.

"Here comes the king," someone said. And, in fact, there was Solomon, along with the Queen of Sheba. From the door, he looked at what was left of the room, where the fire had already been put out. He saw the manuscripts—the work that would consecrate him—all burned up, but he said nothing, manifested no kind of emotion. After all, he was the king, and a king has to keep it on lockdown in front of his subjects, especially a king who aspires to be wise and powerful.

The king looked at me. Yes, now there was sadness in his eyes for the lost writings, but also, and I was sure of it, for me. You were in that text, he was saying to me, your sweat and blood, your passion; I feel for you as much as I feel for myself and the lost work.

When all was said and done, he was a good guy, that Solomon. But he was also the king, and now he needed to fulfill his kingly function.

"What should we do with this individual?" asked the head of security, pointing at the restrained shepherd boy.

Solomon thought for a second. "Let's judge him. Right now."

He turned to the Queen of Sheba. "You wanted a trial, right? Well, now you've got one." He smiled: "Instead of the book I promised you."

Then he declared in a loud voice: "Let us go to the throne room. Everyone."

Off we went. Leading the entourage, the head of security and his guards escorted the shepherd boy. Then Solomon and the Queen of Sheba. Followed by the wives, the concubines, the courtiers. We filed into the throne room. The king slowly climbed the steps to his throne. But he did not sit. There on top, he looked down at the shepherd boy.

"You are accused," he said, in a neutral, deliberate voice, "of having set fire to a palace room, as part of a plot against the king. It is a serious crime. Moreover, it resulted in the destruction of a document of great worth, a document that demanded much toil and effort."

Pause. Complete silence.

"Is this accusation true?" asked the king.

The prisoner did not respond. He simply stared at the king.

"Your silence is equal to an admission of guilt," said Solomon.

Another pause. Everyone anxiously awaited the sentence. Then came the twist:

"I shall not condemn you," said the monarch. A murmur went through the audience like a shock wave, a murmur he silenced by raising his hand. He continued: "You did me no harm. You only managed to cut off your nose to spite your face."

Yet another pause (pauses, by the looks of things, were essential for the gravity, or at least the dramatization, of the verdict), then he went on.

"I would let you go. But I cannot do it. You also destroyed someone's work, and that person has a right to demand that you be punished."

He pointed at me. "You. You will judge him."

Me? Me, judge the shepherd boy? Me, the ugly one, the rejected wife? It was an honor, and everyone looked at me with admiration and envy—but no, who was I to judge? Domine, non sum dignus.

He, meanwhile, insisted, and this time it was an order. "Yes, you. Come, take my place." He descended and came to where I was. He gestured to the staircase. "It's all yours."

There was no way out of it. Slowly, I began to climb the stairs, keeping an eye on the lions. Despite their ferocious appearance, their toothy grins, they remained still. I wasn't afraid that they would merely shake their heads in disapproval—It can't be, not a woman on the throne, and an ugly one to boot—but worse, that they would pounce from their pedestals and block my way: You shall not pass! You shall not pass! But no, the beasts remained still. And they remained so because someone—not the king, but the gear operator—kept them still. Had he heard Solomon's order? Or had he made the decision based on his own judgment? According to legend, the monarch's wisdom was the result of certain books placed under his throne; it was as if wisdom, emanating from the manuscripts, seeped into the sovereign's brain like a vapor. But was it really transmitted in a sort of telepathic mechanism by the lion operator to the king? Could it be that Solomon was little more than an agent of some humble machine operator who never saw the light of day? I would not get an answer to this question. Not right now. I was almost to the throne.

After a brief hesitation, I sat. The seat was cold, penetratingly cold. And the throne was tall, much taller than I had imagined. Up top I felt isolated. It wasn't the same isolation I used to experience when climbing the mountain and contemplating the desert from on high; no, on the throne it was all about the isolation of power. An isolation, a power, I was not prepared for. All the people, hundreds of people, looking at me, awaiting my words. It was truly terrifying. But I couldn't panic, not yet. So I took a deep breath and prepared to pass judgment. Okay, people, where is the infant that needs cutting in half? Let's get to it.

"Come closer," I said to the shepherd boy. He approached the throne. He looked at me with such amazement, with such fear, that it made me want to laugh: What's your problem, man, going around burning manuscripts and then shitting your pants with fear? What's up with that?

"Is it true," I asked, "that you burned the manuscript mentioned by our king, King Solomon?"

(It was an unnecessary question, but it was the only thing that came to mind. At least it would help me buy some time.)

"It's," he stammered. "It's true. I did it. I burned said manuscript."

"Hmm. You burned the manuscript . . . Right on, you did it."

I had learned from the best. Like the king, I made a dramatic pause. And then I declared my verdict, a verdict that surprised even me, because I heard myself speak but it was as if the voice were not my own, as if someone else were speaking through my mouth. Who? Not Solomon's wife, that's for sure; maybe that girl who ran on mountain trails, that girl who, despite her misfortune, feared nothing.

"Set him free. May he lead the Queen of Sheba back to her land."

My words unleashed a real shitstorm: a mix of boos and applause. To my surprise—my gratifying surprise—the women were rapt with joy; the courtiers, on the other hand, were pissed: Go figure, the shame of it, freeing a crook like that. I didn't care. I'd completed my mission and saved the shepherd boy. With tears in his eyes, he looked at me in gratitude. I descended the steps, this time the lions nodding their heads as a sign of approval. I stood by Solomon, who managed to give me a royal wink.

The head of security, still confused, asked what he ought to do with the prisoner.

"Didn't you hear her sentence?" said the king. "That man is free. Let him go."

The guards unlocked the shackles on the shepherd boy's ankles and his one good arm. Someone touched my shoulder. I turned: It was the Queen of Sheba, who wanted to compliment me on my ruling. She confessed that she hadn't understood much, but that she would return to her land impressed.

The trial concluded, we all headed for the palace entrance, where the caravan waited, ready to depart. Solomon and the Queen of Sheba exchanged formal goodbyes befitting of two rulers; no giggling or moaning, no more dirty talk in verse. Cover me with the kisses of your mouth, not a chance. Solomon gave a gentle bow and that was it. As graceful as ever, she walked to the kneeling camel, which waited, chewing its cud. She stepped into the tent and the curtains closed. The shepherd boy, in turn, took his place as guide. He passed by, eyed me, was about to say something but couldn't get it out. The look he gave me, however, said it all. The caravan got under way, applauded by the multitude concentrated in front of the palace. And then it disappeared over a hill.

Having nothing more to do in my destroyed room, I returned to the harem. As I expected, my old bed had been taken; over the past days, and despite all the confusion, Solomon had married two more wives and bought three more concubines from some broke-ass king. Luckily, there was another bed, left behind by an Edomite who'd just passed away. It wasn't as nice, because Edomites were, for some reason, losing their prestige, but I didn't feel like making a fuss. When night came, I collapsed, exhausted.

The harem overseer woke me up from a deep, dreamless sleep. "Solomon is sending for you," she whispered, her eyes bright in the partial darkness.

At first, I didn't understand. Solomon, sending for me? What for? But the woman insisted and, although sleepy, I managed to get out of bed. The woman tried to get me ready, a little makeup, but I refused. I went as I was, hair a mess, me a hot mess—much uglier than normal.

※

Solomon was waiting for me, stretched out on the large bed. He was extremely sweet with me; he had me lie beside him. He caressed me, asked me how I wanted it.

Truth be told, I wanted him to let me sleep, but it was now or never. So: "Cover me with the kisses of your mouth," I said, somewhat timorously. Would the magic words work? Was I not running the risk of more disappointment?

The magic words worked. God, did they work! The guy was good in bed; and I, in my debut, wasn't half bad. My belly was like a goblet, and from my goblet he took a long sip of my impassioned wine. It wasn't the prosaic nuptial night that I had expected; it was a celebration, a real banquet of sex, every position, every technique probed. On a scale of one to ten, an eight, discounted in virtue of my sense of modesty.

I got up early in the morning. He was still asleep, dreaming—about what, I would never know, and I didn't care to: I preferred mystery. I kissed him for the last time and left. I walked quietly through the corridors and came to the garden. The pigeons looked at me from their nooks.

I jumped the palace wall with ease. Running down the sleepy city streets, I headed south, toward the desert. I was after a certain shepherd boy. If I hurried, I could catch him in two or three days. Around a certain mountain. With its enigmatic but promising caves.

CONTRIBUTORS

ABOUT THE AUTHOR

Moacyr Scliar was born in Porto Alegre, Brazil, in 1937. The son of immigrants from Bessarabia, he would become the preeminent literary voice of immigrant and Jewish experiences in Brazil. He completed his studies in medicine at the Federal University of Rio Grande do Sul in 1962. For the next three decades, he worked as a physician in public health, a career that undoubtedly influenced his writing. A prolific writer, Scliar wrote more than seventy books during his lifetime and cultivated a range of genres, including short stories, essays, novels, and children's literature. His notable works include *The Centaur in the Garden* (1980), *Max and the Cats* (1981), *The Strange Nation of Rafael Mendes* (1983), *The Majesty of Xingu* (1997), *The Woman Who Wrote the Bible* (1999), and *Kafka's Leopards* (2000). He won numerous awards, including the Jabuti Award three times (1988, 1993, and 2000) and the Casa de las Américas Award (1989). His *The Centaur in the Garden* was listed among the Hundred Greatest Works of Modern Jewish Literature by the National Yiddish Book Center in the United States. In 1999, *The Collected Stories of Moacyr Scliar* won the National Jewish Book Award. He was inducted into the Brazilian Academy of Letters in 2003. His work has been translated into more than a dozen languages and adapted for film, theater, television, and radio. He passed away in 2011.

ABOUT THE TRANSLATOR

Heath Wing grew up in West Texas and is currently an associate professor of Spanish at North Dakota State University. He specializes in Latin American literatures and literary translation. His translations have appeared in *Brooklyn Rail*, *Asymptote*, *The Common*, *Latin American Literature Today*, *Waxwing*, *International Poetry Review*, and in the anthology *Becoming Brazil*.

ABOUT THE SERIES EDITOR

Ilan Stavans is the Lewis-Sebring Professor of Humanities and Latin American and Latino Culture at Amherst College, the cofounder and publisher of Restless Books, and the academic director of the Great Books Summer Program. The recipient of numerous awards and honors, his work, translated into twenty languages, has been adapted for film, theater, television, and radio.